ROBODOG

Books by David Walliams

THE BOY IN THE DRESS
MR STINK
BILLIONAIRE BOY
GANGSTA GRANNY
RATBURGER
DEMON DENTIST
AWFUL AUNTIE
GRANDPA'S GREAT ESCAPE
THE MIDNIGHT GANG
BAD DAD
THE ICE MONSTER
THE BEAST OF BUCKINGHAM PALACE
CODE NAME BANANAS
GANGSTA GRANNY STRIKES AGAIN!
SPACEBOY

FING
SLIME
MEGAMONSTER
ROBODOG

THE WORLD'S WORST CHILDREN 1
THE WORLD'S WORST CHILDREN 2
THE WORLD'S WORST CHILDREN 3
THE WORLD'S WORST TEACHERS
THE WORLD'S WORST PARENTS
THE WORLD'S WORST PETS

Also available in picture book:

THE SLIGHTLY ANNOYING ELEPHANT
THE FIRST HIPPO ON THE MOON
THE QUEEN'S ORANG-UTAN
THE BEAR WHO WENT BOO!
THERE'S A SNAKE IN MY SCHOOL!
BOOGIE BEAR
GERONIMO
LITTLE MONSTERS
MARMALADE
GRANNYSAURUS

David Walliams

ROBODOG

ILLUSTRATED BY
ADAM STOWER

HarperCollins *Children's Books*

First published in the United Kingdom by
HarperCollins *Children's Books* in 2023
HarperCollins *Children's Books* is a division of HarperCollins*Publishers* Ltd
1 London Bridge Street
London SE1 9GF

www.harpercollins.co.uk

HarperCollins*Publishers*
Macken House, 39/40 Mayor Street Upper
Dublin 1, D01 C9W8, Ireland

1

HB ISBN 978-0-00-846955-9
TPB ISBN 978-0-00-858143-5
PB ISBN 978-0-00-858144-2

For Bert & Ernie,
my two furry bundles of love.

THANK-YOUS

I WOULD LIKE TO THANK...

CALLY
POPLAK
EXECUTIVE PUBLISHER

CHARLIE
REDMAYNE
CEO

ADAM
STOWER
**MY
ILLUSTRATOR**

PAUL
STEVENS
**MY LITERARY
AGENT**

NICK LAKE
MY EDITOR

VAL
BRATHWAITE
**CREATIVE
DIRECTOR**

SALLY GRIFFIN
DESIGNER

ELORINE GRANT
ART DIRECTOR

MATTHEW KELLY
ART DIRECTOR

MEGAN REID
FICTION EDITOR

GERALDINE STROUD
PR DIRECTOR

TANYA HOUGHAM
AUDIO PRODUCER

ALEX COWAN
HEAD OF MARKETING

David Walliams

Have you ever heard of a police cat?

NO!

Of course not!

There is no such thing.

Never has been and never will be.

Police cats would be utterly useless. Cats don't do anything they don't want to do.

Could you train a cat to **MIAOW** at a robber? No.

Could you train a cat to **guard** some jewels? Not likely.

Could you train a cat to chase a criminal? Never!

Could you train a cat to do anything? A BIG FAT **NO.**

Cats are lazy. Cats are selfish. Cats are rude.

Oh! Please don't tell any cats I wrote this about them. If you do, there is every chance that one day you will read that I mysteriously choked on a furball.

Not that I am saying ALL cats are bad. Just ninety-nine per cent of them.

Dogs, however, couldn't be more different from cats.

Dogs are eager to please. Dogs want to be loved. Crucially, dogs will do anything for a treat.

That is why dogs make the perfect partners for police. You see them used by police forces across the world.

As we all know, dogs come in numerous shapes and sizes.

Tiny ones. Huge ones.

Quiet ones. Loud ones.

Weak ones. Strong ones.

Bald ones. Furry ones.

Slow ones. Fast ones.

Now, different types of dogs are good at different jobs. That's why the police train many different breeds for their work.

These are just some of the breeds you will find in training at a **POLICE DOG SCHOOL:**

The powerful German shepherd: perfect for wrestling robbers to the ground.

"OOF!"

The big-nosed bloodhound: highly skilled at following the scents of criminals on the run.

"SNORT!"

The noisy spaniel: no dog could bark louder at baddies.

"WOOF! WOOF! WOOF!"

The superfast greyhound: the speediest breed to run messages between police officers.

WHIZZ!

The ever-eager terrier: always proud to patrol police stations.

TROT-TROT-TROT!

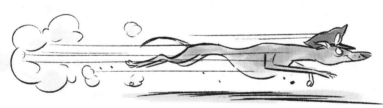

The brave **schnauzer:** this dog would do anything to protect its police-officer partner.

"GRRR!"

The keen-nosed **beagle:** can sniff out any bad things being smuggled in suitcases.

"SNIFF!"

But what if one dog could perform all these tasks and more? They would be the greatest police dog of all time.

Prepare to meet ROBODOG:

the future of crime fighting.

LET'S MEET

THE HEROES

AND

THE VILLAINS

IN THIS STORY...

THE HEROES

THE ROBOT

ROBODOG
Robodog is the greatest police dog ever built.

THE RAT

RATTY

Ratty looks like a rat, smells like a rat and acts like a rat, but is adamant he is a mouse.

THE HUMANS

THE CHIEF

This unusually short lady occupies the giant position of Chief of Police. She oversees the city of Bedlam's police force and takes a special interest in her school for police dogs.

THE PROFESSOR

The professor is the wife of the chief. An inventor, she spends her days in her laboratory in the cellar of their grand old country house Fuzz Manor.

THE GENERAL

The General is the boastful head of the army.

THE DOGS

SCARPER

The nervy one.

GRISTLE
The idle one.

PLANK
The silly one.

THE VILLAINS

THE CATS

VELMA

Velma belongs to the chief and the professor, but she sees it the other way round. They belong to her! She loathes dogs with a deep and dark passion. When a dog enters Fuzz Manor, fur flies.

SLASH

Slash is the most terrifying creature you ever could meet. This cat has a gigantic scar across his face from a fight with a pack of wolves. The wolves lost.

CODGER

This alley cat is so old
nobody can remember how
old he is. Not even him.

PAVAROTTI

Pavarotti is the biggest cat in the world. He
prefers to be pushed around in a wheelbarrow.

THE SUPERVILLAINS

MIGHTY MIND

This master criminal is behind more robberies in the city of Bedlam than anyone else. His body died many years ago, and now he is a giant mega-brain floating in a glass bowl.

HAMMERHANDS

Mighty Mind's henchperson is a short, round lady who has giant hammers instead of hands. She isn't afraid to use them.

THE MASKED HONKER

The Masked Honker is a lady
who farts fire.

BIG BAD BOB

He is the size of a house.
Not a big house, but a
house, nonetheless.

THE CHOCOLATIER
Beware the coffee-flavoured chocolates! They are in his selection box of delights somewhere!

DR STENCH
Her breath is so pongy you would turn green before you died.

THE ICE QUEEN
This regal villainess can turn you to ice with a touch of her little finger.

THE TICKLE MONSTER

A creature with impossibly long arms,
the Tickle Monster can tickle you to death.

THE TWO-HEADED OGRE

It can't agree on anything.

THE WICKED HEADMISTRESS

Her secret weapon is homework, homework and more homework.

THE POLITICIAN

She can bore you to death with just one sentence!

PROFESSOR SQUID

Squirt!

THE GIANT WORM

A giant worm.

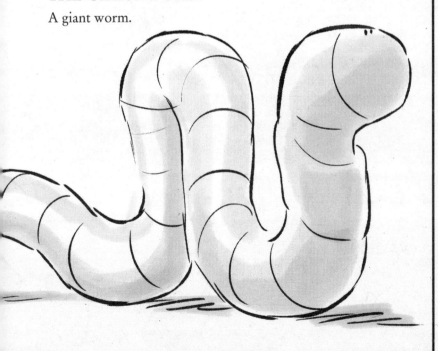

WELCOME TO BEDLAM

ENTER ONLY IF YOU DARE

*B*EDLAM is a city where the underworld has burst up from under the pavements and taken over.

It is cold. It is dark. It is ugly.

The rat-infested urban jungle is not just filthy, but also one of the most dangerous places on Earth. **BEDLAM** has become home to a galaxy of gangsters. They have subjected the good people of the city to a reign of terror. Nothing and nobody is safe from these evil criminals.

The city needs its own **superhero** to defeat the supervillains.

But who?

THE LOST PATROL

BEDLAM was a pustule on the face of the world.

A jungle of crumbling buildings loomed over narrow streets, casting them in eternal shadow.

Rats ran riot.

Trash was piled up on street corners.

The river was a deep shade of brown.

And a thick smog hung over the city like a bad smell.

BEDLAM had once been home to the dreams of ordinary people; now it was a place of *NIGHTMARES.*

The City Jail was overrun with the most wicked criminals of all time, but **BEDLAM** made new ones all the time. The latest evil duo to make the front page of the *Bedlam Bugle* was **MIGHTY MIND** and his henchperson **Hammerhands.**

This was just the latest in a long list of headlines.

BEDLAM may have been a lawless place, but it was not without hope.

The shortest person in the police force was also the most able. When she was a child, she would arrest the bullies in the playground. As soon as she left school, she joined the police force and since then had been on the front line in the fight against crime. The lady was older

now and had finally been made **BEDLAM'S** Chief of Police. She was known simply as 'Chief', even to her wife, who was an inventor she called 'Professor'.

One of the chief's big ideas was to open **BEDLAM'S** first police-dog training school. She was sure dogs could prove to be a powerful weapon to prevent the city's criminals from taking over. To begin with, she had been proved right. Her army of police dogs, paired up with police officers, had brought some of **BEDLAM'S** supervillains to justice. Thanks to those brave dogs, these supervillains were now locked up in **BEDLAM'S** City Jail. However, every week more and more of these supervillains emerged, and sometimes it felt as if the police were losing the battle.

The chief found a deserted army training camp on the outskirts of the city, and had it turned into a school for police dogs.

The parade ground
Just like police officers, the police dogs had a passing-out parade after they had successfully completed their training.

A dog bath
The dogs were representing the police force, and were expected to look their best.

A tree
So the dogs had somewhere to pee.

Kennels
These contained a dozen or so beds. The beds were just the right size for one big dog, or two little ones sleeping top to tail.

A shed
At the far end of the training field squatted a little broken-down shed. It was a pathetic sight, with a flag permanently at half-mast. The flag had "The Lost Patrol" emblazoned across it.

The "Lost Patrol" was the nickname for the trio of dogs who lived in the shed.

They were called that because they had been at the training school for years and years, but had **never** passed. These dogs had to do all their training again and again because they were either too nervy, too lazy or too silly.

Let's meet them:

Scarper

Scarper might have been a huge powerful German shepherd, but he was the nervy one. The poor thing was frightened of a flea.

Plank
The bloodhound was the silly one, and when
I say "silly", I mean super silly. She was so
silly she would forget she was a dog.

Gristle
A beagle. The littlest one was also the idlest.
Gristle would sleep all day if you let him.

All three members of the Lost Patrol were responsible for some of the world's worst **DOG DISASTERS!**

There was the time Scarper was hiding under a chair and accidentally tickled the bottom of the Chief of Police with his tail.

"HA! HA! HA!"

Or the time Gristle stole a police motorcycle so he wouldn't have to take part in the cross-country run.

V R O O M !

Or who can forget the time Plank thought the visiting president was a robber and wrestled him to the ground in front of the entire school?

"ARGH!"

The terrible trio had now been living at the **POLICE DOG SCHOOL** for longer than any of them could remember, especially Plank. Plank could barely remember her own name. However, the chief had high hopes that this year the three might just scrape through and finally be out there patrolling the streets of **BEDLAM**. Fighting crime. Catching the baddies. Being awarded big, shiny medals for their bravery.

How **wrong** she would be.

DOG DISASTERS

Our adventure begins on the morning of the passing-out **parade**. This was the big day when, after completing their training, the recruits finally found out whether they had graduated to be working police dogs.

It was a foggy morning. Cold, damp and dark like most mornings in **BEDLAM**.

However, all the dogs had been groomed to perfection. Fur trimmed. Claws polished. Teeth cleaned. Paws wiped. Bottoms brushed.

Even the Lost Patrol looked presentable.

Scarper had had a bath.

Gristle had licked one of his paws.

And Plank had fallen into the lake.

So, after getting lost on the way to the **parade**

ground not once, not twice, not thrice...

THIS IS GOING TO TAKE TOO LONG!

...BUT **SEVEN TIMES,** the Lost Patrol finally took their places alongside the other dogs for the passing-out **parade**.

"Now that we are all here," began the chief pointedly, glaring at the three late arrivals, "we can finally begin." The peak of the lady's cap was just visible over the lectern. The chief may have been short, but she was **fierce** and always commanded attention.

Cap

Eyes that don't miss a thing

Short, neat hair

Determined look

Tassels

Leather gloves

Row of medals for bravery

Spotless uniform

Black tights

Highly polished shoes

"As you know, this city of **BEDLAM** is home to some of the dastardliest criminals the world has ever known. Just last night, the city's museum was emptied of all its treasures."

The chief held up a copy of the *Bedlam Bugle*. The headline read…

There was a collective gasp from all the dogs.

"**BEDLAM** needs dogs like you to be on the front line of policing like never before. Well done: you have all worked extremely hard in your training over the past year, and are about to finally become police dogs!" said the chief.

The dogs all barked their approval.

"WOOF! WOOF! WOOF!"

"This is not just a proud day for me – it is a proud day for all of you. This is the greatest day of any dog's life. The day you finally become working members of the police force! To pass all your tests makes you the best of the best. You should all give yourselves a jolly good pat on the back!"

It was just a figure of speech. The chief didn't mean they should actually pat themselves on the back. There was just one dog on the **parade** ground who could not understand that.

Plank.

The dog raised her front paw. She tried to pat herself on the back, but it was a lot harder than she had imagined. Then Plank had a go with her back paw. Instantly, she lost her balance and toppled on top of Scarper.

"OOOF!"

Scarper fell on top of Gristle.

"AH!"

And Gristle thudded to the ground.

The beagle was knocked out cold.

DONK!

"The time has come," continued the chief proudly, "to come up one by one, in an orderly fashion, for me to shake your paw and welcome you to the **BEDLAM** Police Force!"

So the dogs stepped forward and formed a line. Now all one hundred dogs were in formation, ready to meet the chief. The dogs were perfectly spaced out, like a row of dominoes waiting to topple.

What could possibly go wrong?

As it turned out... EVERYTHING!

FUR MOUNTAIN

Coming round after being knocked out cold, Gristle went to join the end of the line. Still a bit dazed, he tripped over his own paws.

WALLOP!

Gristle began tumbling towards the end of the queue. His head was where his bottom should be, and his bottom was where his head should be. Therefore, he couldn't see where he was going. Not that it mattered, as he was going too fast to stop himself. He walloped into Scarper, who walloped into Plank, who walloped into the next dog, who walloped into the next...

Soon a hundred dogs were tumbling on top of each other.

They were surging forward together. An unstoppable force! A TIDAL WAVE OF DOGS! Noses. Legs. Ears. Tongues. Paws. Tails. Bellies. Backs. Bottoms. All were tangled up together.

The chief cried out
"STOP!" as they
headed straight for her.
But the dogs
couldn't stop even
if they'd wanted to.
In a moment, the chief
was buried under a FUR
MOUNTAIN!

THWUMP!

The pile of a hundred
dogs and one lady was as
tall as the school watchtower.

"WOOF! WOOF! WOOF!"

barked the dogs as they tried to wriggle
off each other. Right at the very bottom,
with a bottom in her face (not of the
human kind, but of the dog kind)
was the chief.

When she finally emerged with a little dog perched on her head, the lady was fuming.

Her face was scarlet with **Fury** and steam was coming out of her ears.

The lady's immaculate uniform was dirty and torn to shreds.

"THAT'S IT!" cried the chief. "YOU HAVE **ALL** FAILED! NONE OF YOU WILL BECOME POLICE DOGS THIS YEAR!"

All eyes turned to Gristle.

"**GRRR!**" growled the dogs angrily.

Gristle looked around as if they couldn't possibly mean him.

"Is it something I said?" he asked innocently.

From that moment on, the Lost Patrol became outcasts. The other dogs blamed them bitterly. Now they would all have to do another year of training.

IT WAS A **CATASTROPHE.**

All three members of the Lost Patrol found themselves being picked on.

Their ears were nibbled.

Their treats were stolen.

Their shed was peed on.

Their toys were mauled.

Their water bowls were kicked over.

Their tails were yanked.

Their collars were chewed.

Their paws were tickled.

Their bones were buried.

Worst of all, their food was farted on!

DUM! DUM! DUM!

I told you it was **bad.**

"Is it me or are all the other dogs being a bit funny with us?" asked Gristle.

"Yes. They've all been so nice!" replied Plank.

"NO! THEY HAVEN'T!" shouted Scarper. "They have all been horrible to us!"

The three dogs were in their little shed at the far end of the **parade** ground. As always, the sad-looking flag with the words "The Lost Patrol" flew at half-mast from a pole on the roof.

"I thought my breakfast had a different flavour," piped up Plank.

"Yes! It did! A farty flavour!" replied Gristle.

"Can you buy it in the tin like that?" asked Plank.

"No! You can't buy it like that!" exclaimed Scarper.

"Shame," remarked Plank.

"Don't you understand?" cried Scarper. "All our food has been farted on! The other dogs are doing everything they can possibly do to make our lives a misery!"

"Whatever for?" asked Gristle.

"For what you did!" replied Scarper. "Making us all tumble over each other and end up in a huge fur mountain on top of the Chief of Police!"

"That was MY fault?" asked an innocent-looking Gristle.

"YES!"

Gristle covered his eyes with his paw, hopped over to the corner of the shed and fell on to his side.

THUMP!

Then he whimpered, as he was feeling mightily sorry for himself.

"HMMM!"

Little did the Lost Patrol know that the worst was yet to come.

THE EVILLEST CAT IN THE WORLD

Meanwhile, on the other side of **BEDLAM**, the chief was racing home in her police car. The lady was so covered in dog hair she looked like a Yeti.

SPOT THE DIFFERENCE

CHIEF OF POLICE

YETI

The chief had been humiliated. This could never, ever happen again. Her mind was racing as fast as her car. There must be another way!

As soon as she arrived back at her grand country house on the edge of a cliff – **Fuzz Manor** – the chief called for her wife. Instantly,

the professor raced up from her **LABORATORY** and went to work with her roller to try to remove all the dog hair from the chief's uniform. The professor was a boffin and dressed like one too.

Wild hair

Cake crumbs

Leaky ink pen in pocket

Singed laboratory coat

Glasses on a chain

Odd socks

Tea stains

Sandals

The professor spent her days in a LABORATORY in the cellar of **ᖴᑌᘔᘔ Mᴀnor**. It was a sea of test tubes, Bunsen burners and lengths of rubber tubing. The professor had become celebrated for inventing a super-duper washing machine that only took one minute to wash and dry your clothes. Still, she was always looking to build something bigger and better.

"Just a tiny bit more. Just a tiny bit more. Just a tiny bit more," said the professor with each roll of her roller.

"You keep on saying that!" snapped the chief, still coated in a deep layer of hair.

"Hold still!"

"I *am* holding still! You are just moving the fur around."

"No! I'm not! Look!" exclaimed the professor. She held up the roller, which now resembled a giant fur lollipop.

"Harrumph!" harrumphed the chief.

From the sofa, Velma looked on at the scene

with disdain. Velma was a cat, or rather, a huge grey ball of fur with four legs and a tail sticking out of it. Like most cats, Velma ruled the roost at the home the two ladies shared.

And this cat *hated* dogs.

Cats and dogs had been sworn enemies since the dawn of time, but Velma was different. Velma was the evillest cat in the world. She wanted to rid the world of dogs forever. Velma spent her days perched dead still on the garden wall, waiting for any dogs to pass by. When they did,

she would summon up the biggest, roundest furball and fire it straight at them like a missile.

COUGH!

WHOOSH!

"YELP!"

Then she would smirk and bare her fangs, and the dogs would scurry away in fear, howling.

"AROO!"

Velma was a clever cat. She knew dog hair when she saw it, and it had no place in HER home. So she waited and waited until the professor held the fur-covered roller aloft, and chose that moment to let rip a hurricane of a sneeze.

"ACHOOOOOOOOOOOOO!"

The force of the sneeze was so great that the mass of fur shot off the roller and landed right in the professor's face.

WHOOSH!

It looked as if she had transformed into a werewolf.

"TEE! HEE! HEE!" sniggered the cat.

"I have been thinking," began the chief.

"That's not like you," joked the professor as she plucked the hairs one by one from her face.

The two ladies had been together for all their grown-up lives. They loved each other deeply, but that didn't stop them from teasing one another from time to time. It just made them love each other more.

"Harrumph!" harrumphed the chief again.

"Do go on…"

"When I was lying at the bottom of a tonne of dogs, I had an idea."

"Oh! Pray tell!"

"As you know, at the police force, we have all these different breeds of dogs to perform different jobs."

"Of course."

"But why not just have one dog to do them all?"

"Because there is no dog in the world that can be a sniffer dog AND a guard dog AND a chasing dog!"

"No. Not yet! But you could make one."

"Me?"

"Yes. You are a boffin, aren't you, Professor?"

The professor looked down at her white LABORATORY coat, odd socks and sandals. "It appears so!"

"Well, my thought was that you could design and build a robot police dog!"

"A *what* what?" spluttered the professor.

"The cheek of it!" hissed Velma to herself. "The bare-faced cheek! A dog! In a cat household! NEVER!"

"A robot police dog!" repeated the chief. "One dog to sniff and guard and chase and do all the things a police dog can do and more. And we can call it... ROBODOG!"

The professor could not believe her ears. "I make washing machines! Not robot dogs!"

"Well, it's all the same, isn't it?" suggested the chief.

"Would you trust a dog to wash your smalls?"

"No."

"If you threw a stick, do you think a washing machine would fetch it for you?"

The chief thought for a moment before answering: "No."

"Then it's not all the same now, is it?" replied the professor, folding her arms.

The chief paused and smiled. There must be a way to appeal to the love of her life. "Not exactly the same, no, but you are such a genius, my darling Professor, I just know you can do it!"

"But—"

"The president himself called me this morning to say that if I can't sort out **BEDLAM'S** crime wave for good, he would send in the army."

"The army!"

"It is humiliating!" said the chief. "I have given this city my blood, sweat and tears!"

"No one has done more to fight crime in this city than you."

"So will you please help, my darling, darling wife? **BEDLAM** needs you!"

The professor sighed. "I will do my best."

The chief wrapped her arms round her. "I LOVE YOU!"

EPISODE FIVE

SECRET LABORATORY

The professor hurried down the long spiral staircase into the cellar of the country house. There, in her secret **LABORATORY**, she instantly set to work.

Designing. Building. Programming.

As the professor had created the world's fastest washing machine, she had thousands of parts left over for her new creation.

Buttons

Switches

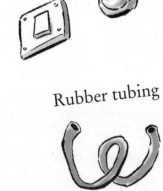

Belts

Rubber tubing

Nuts

Bolts

Glass screens

Sheets of metal

Electric
cables

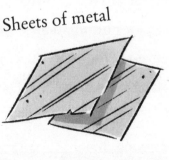

Circuit
boards

Anything she didn't have, like weapons, for example (washing machines rarely have missiles), the chief was dispatched to source.

Although she was a genius inventor, the professor had never made a robot before, let alone a robot dog, or indeed a robot police dog. However, she excelled at the task. She worked day and night on her invention.

Days passed.

Weeks passed.

Months passed.

Sometimes, when the professor's back was turned, Velma would sneak down into the LABORATORY. Lurking in the shadows, the cat would silently observe the woman at work as she was putting all the pieces together with precision.

"I will destroy this robot dog if it is the last thing I do!" hissed Velma to herself.

One time, when the professor was returning from a bathroom break, Velma rushed past her on the stairs on her way out.

"VELMA!" called the professor, very nearly knocked over by this speeding ball of fur.

However, the cat did not stop or make a sound. It looked as if Velma had something in her mouth, but she was going so fast it was impossible to be sure.

All the time, pressure was building on the chief. **BEDLAM** was becoming more and more lawless. **MIGHTY MIND** and **Hammerhands** were terrorising the city with their crime spree.

Finally, the moment came when the professor was ready to unveil her creation. It was the middle of the night when she finally finished building Robodog. She rushed upstairs to wake up her wife, who was fast asleep in bed with Velma lying on her head.

"WAKE UP!" cried the professor, shaking the lady.

"HISS!" hissed Velma as she slid off the chief's head.

The chief opened her eyes and reached for her bedside clock. "It's the middle of the night! Has the whole of **BEDLAM** been destroyed? If not, it can wait until the morning!"

"No!" cried the professor. "I have finished! Come and see!"

With that, the professor dragged the chief, who was dressed in her stripy pyjamas, down the stairs.

Velma followed at a discreet distance.

When the professor and the chief were down in the cellar, the professor pulled a sheet off her creation like a magician and exclaimed,

"TA-DA! PLEASE WELCOME TO THE WORLD... ROBODOG!"

The chief's eyes widened in wonder as she gazed at the robot dog.

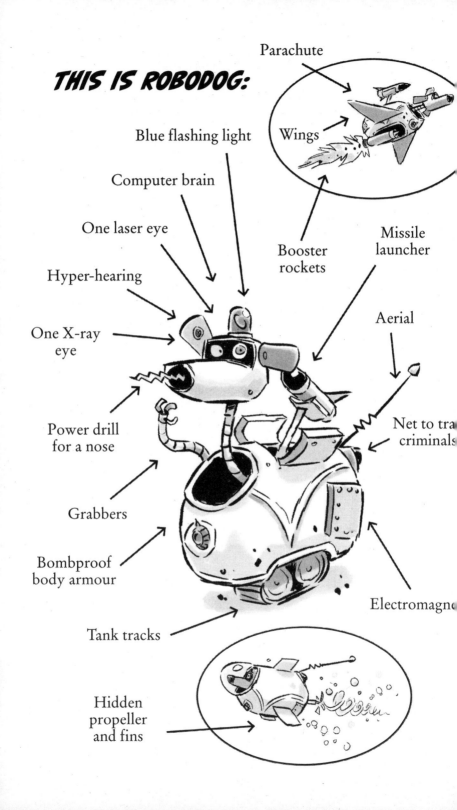

"YOU ARE A GENIUS!" the chief exclaimed, hugging her wife and planting kisses all over her face. "MWAH! MWAH! MWAH!"

"Steady on!" replied the professor.

"But don't you see? Robodog could be the answer to all my prayers! It can not only replace my troublesome police dogs, but take on all of BEDLAM'S supervillains too!"

THE UNTHINKABLE

The professor and the chief stood over the robot dog like proud parents.

"You did it!" said the chief.

"*We* did it!" said the professor.

"Yes! I suppose Robodog was my idea, but I couldn't have done it without little old you!"

The professor rolled her eyes and then smiled.

All the time, spying from the top of the spiral staircase, was Velma.

"HISS!"

The cat viewed the chief and the professor as, at best, uninvited guests in HER house – at worst, squatters. Now they had done the unthinkable! They had brought a DOG into HER house!

The cat often looked as if she were in a foul mood, but right now she scowled a scowl that could crack a mirror!

Her ears stuck up.

Her fangs *flashed*.

Her nostrils **flared.**

Her claws shot out.

Her tail pointed up in such a perfectly straight line that you could have used it as a ruler.

"Do you want to turn it on, my d-d-darling?" asked the professor, her hands trembling with anticipation as she pointed to the button.

"Why are you n-n-nervous?"

"I have created life! It's not just a washing machine – it is something that can think!"

The chief was silent for a moment. "Can it feel too?"

"It's a 'he'!"

"Oh! Can he feel too?"

"I don't know," replied the professor. "I didn't give him a **heart.**"

"So he can't feel?"

A look of deep concern crossed the professor's face. "Maybe this is a bad idea. Maybe I should never have done this."

"Nonsense!"

"I feel nervous about bringing him to life. Let's switch him on together."

"Splendid idea! You first!"

The professor shook her head. "Together!"

Then the pair linked hands and guided their fingers towards the button as one.

KERPLUNK!

At first nothing happened.

Then, after a moment, there were *whirrs* and clicks from deep within the robot.

Next, an eye flickered. Then another.

The nose twitched.

The jaw dropped open.

Then the tail flicked up.

TWANG!

Suddenly, the tracks began turning.

WHIRR!

Robodog trundled at speed across the **LABORATORY**, crashing into a table...

SMASH!

...knocking over a chair...

THUNK!

…and heading straight into a wall.

DOOF!

"He's out of control!" shouted the chief.
"MALFUNCTION! MALFUNCTION! MALFUNCTION!" blurted Robodog.
"TEE! HEE! HEE!" snorted Velma.

UNDER ARREST

"**M**AKE HIM STOP!" cried the professor, as she could see her greatest creation and her LABORATORY being destroyed all at once.

BISH! BASH! BOSH!

"MALFUNCTION! MALFUNCTION! MALFUNCTION!" Robodog kept repeating.

"How do I make him stop?!" exclaimed the chief.

"I don't know! You are the Chief of Police! Arrest him!"

"Arrest him? He's a robot!"

"TEE! HEE! HEE!" sniggered the cat at the chaos she had caused. "This thing will be in the dustbin before the night is out!"

However, Velma was about to get her just

deserts, because Robodog reversed towards the spiral staircase at the speed of a roller-coaster.

WHIZZ!

CLONK!

The staircase wobbled violently, and the cat toppled off.

"MIAOW!"

she screamed as she plummeted through the air.

WHOOSH!

Velma landed right on Robodog's back.

WHOOMPH!

Her claws sprang out.

CLINK! CLINK! CLINK!

"ROBODOG IS UNDER ATTACK FROM A CAT!" blurted the robot.

Velma tried to sink her claws into Robodog's back. Even though they were sharper than a knife, they were no match for the bombproof metal. They couldn't get a grip on him!

Velma was slipping and sliding as the robot dog spun round and round the room, chasing his tail.

WHIRR!

Soon he was nothing but a blur.

WHIZZ!

"CAT! YOU ARE UNDER ARREST!" barked Robodog in his mechanical voice. "CAT! YOU ARE UNDER ARREST! CAT! YOU ARE UNDER ARREST!"

He spun out of control, slamming against a stool, sending Velma flying.

"MIAOW!"

The cat soared through the air...

WHIZZ!

...landing in a bin.

CLANK!

"MIAOW!"

Velma hissed with **Fury**. "NOOOOOOO!" She leaped up out of the bin and on to a worktop. She shook all the bits of rubbish off before flinging herself at the robot dog in a KUNG-FU ATTACK!

"MIAOW!"

As she sailed towards him, Robodog spun round, presenting his metal bottom to the cat.

"CAT! DO NOT MOVE! YOU ARE UNDER ARREST!"

A look of confusion crossed Velma's face. You can hardly blame her. It is hard to not move while you are flying through the air.

Then…

BLAST!

…a rope net shot out of Robodog's bottom!

All the professor and the chief could do was look on as the horror unfolded.

The net hit the flying cat and wrapped itself round her.

THWOMPH!

She dropped like a stone and hit the ground with a THUD!

"**MIAOW!**" cried Velma as she fought to escape. But the more she fought, the more tangled in the net she became. Soon she was all in a jumble.

"HISS!"

Velma poked herself in the eye with her own tail.

"YEOW!" she cried.

She kicked herself in the chin with her paw…

"OOF!"

…before her nose ended up being squashed into her own bottom.

"EURGH!"

All the time, Robodog was circling her at speed.

"CAT! YOU ARE UNDER ARREST!

CAT! YOU ARE UNDER ARREST! CAT! YOU ARE UNDER ARREST!"

"TURN THE BLASTED THING OFF, DEAR!" thundered the chief as she tried to dodge Robodog so she could untangle their cat from the net.

"I AM TRYING, DEAR!" snapped the professor, as she chased after her creation.

Now Robodog was moving so haphazardly it was impossible to catch him.

"PLEASE! I BEG YOU! STOP!" shouted the professor as more of her **LABORATORY** was destroyed. Washing machines old and new were smashed.

CRASH!

They toppled to the floor.

KER-THUNK!

There was only one thing for it. As he came straight towards her, the professor leaped on to Robodog's back.

"HERE GOES!"

THWUNT!

Despite her bulk, there was still no stopping him. Now she was surfing! Surfing a robot dog! Knees bent, arms stretched out for balance, eyes betraying her

BLIND TERROR!

"NOOOOO-OOOOO!"

she cried.

Meanwhile, the chief was fighting to untangle the cat from the net.

"HOLD STILL, VELMA!"

The more she tried to help, the more Velma struggled.

"MIAOW!"

Now the pair were rolling around on the **LABORATORY** floor.

Across the room, the chief's and the professor's eyes locked. Both could see what was about to happen, but neither could do anything to stop it.

They were on a COLLISION COURSE!

All four smashed into each other…

THWACK!

…and found themselves being hurled to each corner of the **LABORATORY**.

BOOF!

PLOMP!

DUMPH!

CLANK!

Robodog ended up lying on his back, looking like an upside-down tortoise.

"CAT! YOU ARE UNDER ARREST! CAT! YOU ARE UNDER ARREST! CAT! YOU ARE UNDER ARREST!"

His tracks were still running.

WHIRR!

The chief scrambled across the floor and finally flicked Robodog's switch to OFF.

"CAT! YOU ARE UNDER ARR—!"

CLUNK!

Meanwhile, the professor crawled over to the cat. With a pair of scissors, she cut Velma out of the net.

"MIAOW!"

The evil creature rewarded her owner with a deep scratch across her hand.

SCRATCH!

"OUCH!" cried the professor.

"What's the matter?" asked the chief, dashing over.

SITTING ON A FREEZING-COLD TOILET SEAT

LISTENING TO SUPER-LOUD HEAVY METAL MUSIC

BEING HIT ON THE HEAD BY A FOOTBALL

A SNOWBALL SLIDING DOWN THE BACK OF YOUR NECK

TREADING ON LEGO BAREFOOT

"Velma just scratched me!" she replied, holding up her bleeding hand as evidence. "She drew blood!"

"BAD CAT!"

Velma bared her fangs and hissed: **"HISS!"**

Then, to be not just bad but **wicked,** the cat bit deep into the chief's earlobe.

The pain was off the scale.

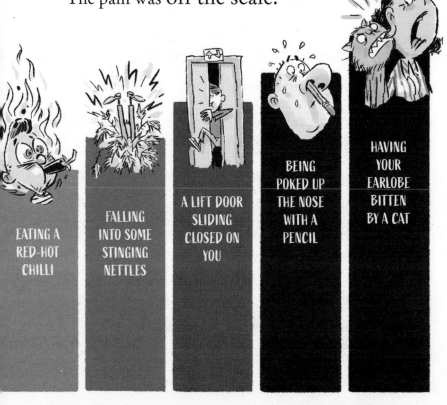

EATING A RED-HOT CHILLI

FALLING INTO SOME STINGING NETTLES

A LIFT DOOR SLIDING CLOSED ON YOU

BEING POKED UP THE NOSE WITH A PENCIL

HAVING YOUR EARLOBE BITTEN BY A CAT

"AAARRRGHHH!" screamed the chief, as well you might if your earlobe were bitten by a cat.

Velma shot back up the spiral staircase, and the professor and the chief were left alone in the **LABORATORY**.

"Robodog is more of a menace than a real dog," huffed the chief. "You can sell him off for scrap metal!"

"No! No! No!" pleaded the professor. "There was just a little problem."

"A big problem! A huge problem! A ginormous problem!"

"A tiny piece was missing from his brain."

"I would say the whole brain was missing!"

"That piece controls his behaviour. I need to take Robodog apart again to see what is wrong."

"I can't have this thing creating chaos in the city! **BEDLAM** already has more than enough of that!"

"I know! I promise I will have Robodog working perfectly soon."

"Hmmm…" mused the chief, not the least bit convinced.

"**HISS!**" hissed Velma from the top of the staircase.

Cat and dog relations had got off to a terrible start.

EPISODE EIGHT

LITTER TRAY

So that night the professor took Robodog to pieces to see what had gone so disastrously wrong. Only when she examined the computer that was the robot's brain did she realise that her suspicion was correct. An important piece was missing. The strangest thing was that the professor distinctly remembered placing this piece there. Perhaps it had popped out somehow as Robodog ran riot. However, she turned her **LABORATORY** upside down searching for it and still couldn't find it.

Admitting defeat, she clambered up the now-wonky spiral staircase that led back into the house.

"I need a cup of coffee!" she muttered to herself.

Trudging through the kitchen like a zombie, due to a lack of sleep, she stepped in Velma's litter tray.

THWUNK!

The little pellets
of litter flew up
into the air.

However, in the grey storm, something glinted in the light.

It fell to the kitchen floor with a CLINK!

Intrigued, the professor sank to her knees and searched for this tiny piece of treasure. Buried under the pellets was exactly the piece of Robodog's brain she'd been looking for all along! A tiny, crucial circuit board that regulated the robot dog's behaviour.

"How on earth did this end up in Velma's litter tray?" the professor asked herself. "Velma?"

The cat didn't make a sound. Once again, she was lurking in the shadows, spying on the professor, this time from on top of a cupboard.

"Darn! My secret is out!" whispered Velma to herself. She had stolen the circuit board nights before in an act of SABOTAGE! Having spied on her mistress at work, Velma knew Robodog was a complex creation. He was made from thousands of tiny little pieces, all intricately put together. If just one of those were missing, she knew Robodog would MALFUNCTION. That was, of course, exactly what had happened. "But I will have my REVENGE on that metal mutt!"

The professor leaped to her feet holding the piece, and all but hurled herself down the staircase to her **LABORATORY** below.

"EUREKA!" she exclaimed.

Her hands trembling with anticipation, the professor put Robodog back together. With the precision of a brain surgeon, she placed the missing circuit board in exactly the right spot. Then she took a deep breath and flicked Robodog's switch to **ON**.

CLICK!

Was her greatest creation going to wreak havoc again?

Robodog's eyes flickered into life.

His nose twitched.

And his tail stood upright.

TWANG!

"My name is Robodog," he began. "Welcome to the future of crime fighting. What are your orders, please?"

The professor beamed with delight. He was perfect!

At the top of the staircase, Velma was snooping again.

"This thing!" she hissed. "In MY house. I will destroy you, Robodog! I will destroy you if it's the last thing I do!"

Then the cat let out a little chuckle. Not that what she'd said was funny, far from it. Rather, she had seen villains in films do it and felt it was the right thing to do.

"HUH! HUH! HUH!"

She laughed a little too hard and coughed up a furball.

SPLUTT!

The sound made Robodog look up. "A cat!" he said to Velma. "I am programmed to love cats! I am Robodog! What is your name, please?"

"Velma! And I am not programmed to love dogs!"

"I am sure we can be friends!" chirped the robot.

The professor looked on. She couldn't understand what they were saying to each other but was delighted that they were speaking. "How wonderful to see you two getting along so well! Just wait until I tell the chief!"

The professor hurried up the spiral staircase, leaving the two animals alone.

"Good to meet you, Velma!" said Robodog. "How do you—"

"Goodbye, Robodog!" replied Velma.

With that, the cat hopped out of the **LABORATORY** and slammed the heavy wooden door behind her.

SLAM!

The key was in the lock, so she hastily turned it...

CLICK!

...and swallowed it.

GULP!

"Goodbye forever!" she hissed.

But then she noticed a red beam of light burning through the door. In moments, a robot-dog-shaped outline had been cut in it, and the smouldering piece of the door fell through.

THUNT!

Robodog breezed through the hole, his laser eye still glowing **red.**

"That was a good game, Velma!" he chirped. "What shall we play next?"

"**HISS!**" hissed the cat.

A FLYING DOG

After what had happened the first time Robodog came to life, the chief was adamant that he needed to be put through his paces at the **POLICE DOG SCHOOL**. Despite the professor's assurances that her genius invention was ready for service, the chief put her foot down. There was no way this robot dog was going to be allowed on the dangerous streets of **BEDLAM** without being properly tried and tested.

So the pair left **Fuzz Manor** in stony silence in the chief's police car, with Robodog sitting in the back.

"What should I call you?" asked Robodog, staring at the professor. "Are you my mother?"

The professor didn't know what to say, so

the chief leaped in.

"NO!" snapped the chief. "You are to call her 'Professor', and me 'Chief'."

"Good morning, Chief. Good morning, Professor."

"Good morning, Robodog!" the professor replied.

The chief only sighed.

The professor patted her creation. "Good boy!" she said.

The chief shook her head in disbelief.

"What?" asked the professor.

"You know!"

"I don't!"

The car raced through the city before it zoomed through the gates of the **POLICE DOG SCHOOL**.

"For now, you stay here behind the barracks with Robodog," ordered the chief.

"Yes, ma'am!" replied the professor, giving her wife a mock salute.

The chief was not amused. "I am going to speak for a few moments and then I will give the signal for when Robodog is to appear!"

"Can he make a big entrance?" asked the professor.

"Not too big, please! I don't want to startle the dogs!"

"Of course!" replied the professor, secretly winking at Robodog.

As the chief strode off, the professor bent down to pat her creation.

"Who says I can't pat you?"

Robodog arched his metal neck to make the most of his ears being tickled.

"Can you feel that?" she asked.

"Yes."

"How does it feel?"

"I don't know."

"I am being silly!" The professor withdrew her hand.

"Professor?"

"Yes."

"Are you my mother?"

The professor shifted uneasily in her sandals. Before she could answer…

DRING!

…she was saved by the bell!

It was a signal for all the dogs to make their way to the **parade** ground.

As usual, the Lost Patrol were the last to arrive.

The professor and Robodog stayed out of sight as the chief stood on a box to address the hundred dogs.

"Now, after the fiasco of last year's passing-out **parade**..." began the little lady.

"I dunno what she's talking about," piped up Plank.

"SHUSH!" shushed the other dogs angrily.

"...I have decided to introduce a brand-new breed to the ranks of police dogs," she continued.

There were murmurs from all the dogs.

"WOOF!"

A new breed of dog? Whatever could she mean?

"A dog that can do all the jobs a police dog can do, and more!"

Now there were gasps!

"WOOF!"

"A dog that may one day put all of you dogs out of a job!"

That was IT! The dogs couldn't control their consternation for a moment longer! They all began howling.

"AROOOOOOOOOOO!"

"SILENCE!" shouted the chief.

"AROOOOOOOOOOOOOOO OOOOOOOOOO!"

A police officer handed the chief a megaphone.

"SILENCE!" she ordered.

Finally, the dogs fell silent.

"It is time for you to meet the future of policing: a police dog that I pray may wipe out crime in this cursed city of **BEDLAM** forever! MEET ROBODOG!"

All the dogs looked left and right to catch the first glimpse of this superdog, but he was nowhere to be seen.

Then a *GIANT WHOOSH* was heard overhead.

WHOOSH!

All at once, a hundred pairs of eyes looked up.

115

A metal dog had blasted high into the sky!

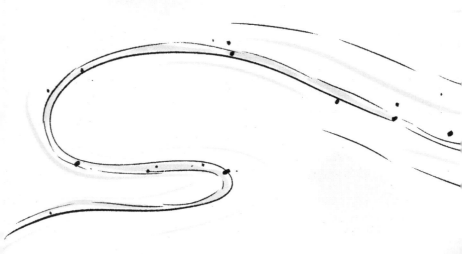

Now its wings were out, and it was soaring through the clouds.

The professor looked up at him proudly.

The dogs' jaws dropped open and their tongues lolled to the ground.

A FLYING DOG!

No one looked more lost than the Lost Patrol.

"What is it?" asked Plank.

"Is it a bird? Is it a plane?" guessed Gristle.

"It looks like some kind of dog," replied Scarper.

"Funny-looking dog," piped up Gristle.

"I know!" began Plank. "It looks like a washing machine! But washing machines can't fly, can they?"

In fairness, Robodog did look a little like a flying washing machine. He was built from spare parts of them, after all.

"You fool! Why would a washing machine take to the sky?" asked Scarper.

"A very fast spin cycle?" guessed Plank.

Robodog descended to the **parade** ground, *zooming* past the assembled dogs, a rather smug look on his metal face.

He came to a perfect stop on the ground.

The professor burst into wild applause. **"GO, ROBODOG! GO! GO! GO!"** she chanted as she danced and clapped her hands like a cheerleader.

"Professor, please!" chided the chief. "Control yourself!"

"Apologies."

Robodog's wings retracted into his

body. Then his tracks began turning, and he took pride of place next to the chief.

"Good morning, Chief of Police!" he chirped. "And may I say how **radiant** you are looking today?"

"What a creep!" remarked Scarper.

"Why, thank you," replied the chief to Robodog, glowing red. Then she turned her attention to the assembled dogs. "Dogs, I want you to welcome to the school, ROBODOG!"

The dogs said nothing. They hated this thing on sight.

"Robodog!" scoffed Scarper. "Stupid name! Why not Dogbot?"

"Or Doggybotty?" suggested Gristle.

"Or Barbara?" added Plank. "It's a lovely name for a dog. I've always wanted to be called Barbara!"

"Robodog has a hundred times the **powers** of a normal dog!" continued the chief. "He can run faster than you, he can **think** faster than you and, most of all, he can follow orders better than you."

"What are your orders, Chief?" asked Robodog.

Climbing frame

Tunnel

Ladders

The chief looked around the school, and her eyes were drawn to the assault course. It was a true test for any dog.

Pond

See-saw

Hurdles

Hoops

"Robodog! Please show your fellow dogs how to conquer the assault course!"

"With pleasure, Chief," he replied.

Then a hatch opened on his back and a missile launcher popped out.

WHOOSH!

The missile shot through the air and

KABOOM!

The assault course exploded!

In an instant, it was a ball of flames.

"Mission accomplished, Chief!" chirped Robodog.

"Not quite what I had in mind," said the chief.

The professor stepped out of her hiding place behind the barracks.

"Might need some clearer orders next time, Chief!" she suggested.

CHALLENGING CHALLENGES

*L*ater that day, the police dogs were set a series of challenges by the chief. The professor stayed to observe, praying there wouldn't be another assault-course-explosion incident.

"Now, dogs, this first challenge of all your three challenges," announced the chief, "is chasing a robber."

"Let's all show this metal menace who's boss!" said Gristle.

"WOOF!" barked the other dogs in agreement.

"Well, when I say 'all', I mean everyone except me," replied Gristle.

A police officer who had clearly drawn the short straw waddled into view, wearing a huge padded suit. He looked as if he'd been inflated. This was to protect him from any dog bites as he was pretending to be a robber. The "robber" was then given a head start before the chief blew a whistle for the dogs to give chase.

TOOT!

The dogs shot off, looking back at Robodog still on the starting line. But Robodog could afford to take his time, because he was the fastest dog the world had ever known.

"WINGS: OUT! BOOSTER ROCKET: FIRE!" he chirped.

Immediately, he transformed into a flying machine and took off with a…

BOOM!

Robodog soared over the heads of all of the dogs giving chase.

ZOOM!

"WOOF! WOOF! WOOF!"

Then a hatch opened on the robot dog's back and his grabbers popped out.

CLUNK!

The arms of the grabbers extended and extended until they reached the "robber".

"ROBBER! YOU ARE UNDER ARREST!" announced Robodog.

Then the grabbers grabbed hold of the back of the man's padded suit and scooped him up into the sky.

WHOOSH!

"I SURRENDER!" cried the policeman.

All the other dogs could do was stop and stare at this magnificent display of police work. The man dangled helplessly in the air, waving his arms and legs, unable to escape Robodog's clutches. He was dragged through the tops of the trees...

RUSTLE! RUSTLE! RUSTLE!

...before he was dropped into the arms of a waiting police officer below.

"OOF!"

"Mission accomplished!" chirped Robodog.

"BRAVO, MY BOY!" shouted the professor

from the sidelines. "BRAVO!"

All the other dogs huffed, none louder than the Lost Patrol. This robot dog was showing them up something rotten.

"Now this next challenge is quite a –" began the chief before pausing, searching for a word she never found – "challenge! You can see that my fellow police officers have placed one hundred suitcases here in a huge pile on the **parade** ground. The challenge is to find the one with the stick of dynamite hidden inside!"

The dogs lurched forward, their noses twitching to sniff out the explosives.

"Wait for it, dogs. You go on my signal!"

TOOT! went the whistle.

"Did I miss catching the robber?" asked the idle Gristle.

The dogs began leaping all over the suitcases, sniffing like crazy.

SNIFF! SNIFF! SNIFF!

Meanwhile, Robodog stood still. He used his

X-ray eye and scanned the hundreds of suitcases in seconds. Instantly, he found the big brown one containing the stick of dynamite.

PING!

"STAND BACK!" he ordered.

All the dogs scampered off. Scarper went one stage further and started frantically digging a hole in which to hide.

Then, with his laser eye, Robodog blasted the suitcase.

ZAP!

KABOOM!

There was a huge explosion. When the smoke cleared, all the other dogs discovered they had turned black with soot.

"GRRR!" they growled.

"Another mission accomplished," chirped the robot.

"OH YEAH! OH YEAH! HE DONE IT! HE DONE IT!" chanted the professor, doing a little victory dance.

"Will you be quiet?" snapped the chief. "You are embarrassing me in front of all the dogs!"

"Sorry."

"Thank you."

"BUT HE DONE IT! HE DONE IT!"

"QUIET! Right, dogs, this final challenge is, in a word, very challenging."

"That's two words," replied the professor.

"QUIET! Now, one of the jobs of police dogs is keeping the citizens of this city safe. You must save someone from drowning!"

On the chief's signal, a police helicopter hovered overhead.

WHIRR!

Dangling from a line under the helicopter was a battered old police car with an officer in a life jacket in the driving seat. He had drawn an even shorter straw. As the helicopter reached the centre of the lake, the line was released.

WHIP!

The car landed in the lake with a giant PLOP!

It began sinking under the water.

BLUB! BLUB! BLUB!

"We've got him now!" exclaimed Scarper.

"Robodog can't get wet! He'll rust!"

"Which one is Robodog again?" asked Plank, the silly one.

The chief blew her whistle.

TOOT!

Scarper dipped his little toe in the water, but decided it was far too cold for him to get in.

Gristle thought it best to sit this one out. It had been an awfully long day.

Meanwhile, Plank had confused a puddle for the lake and had dived into that instead.

SPLAT!

But all the other dogs took a running jump into the water…

SPLOOSH!

…as Robodog stayed on dry land.

The dogs raced to reach the sinking car and drag the man to safety.

"Submarobodog mode: engage!" chirped Robodog.

The robot began to transform again – this time into a submarine.

SWIVEL!

The tracks disappeared up inside his body before fins and a propeller popped out.

CLUNK!

"Transformation complete! Ready to launch!"

"Well, I never," remarked the chief.

Then the robot toppled into the lake…

SPLOOSH!

…and powered under the water.

WHIRR!

Above him, he spotted hundreds of little furry legs doing their best doggy paddle. However, all those dogs were no match for **Submarobodog,** who whooshed past them.

He reached the sinking car in moments, dived down underneath it and engaged his super-strong electromagnet from his tummy.

BUZZ!

Immediately, the bottom of the car stuck to the electromagnet.

CLUNK!

Still deep underwater, **Submarobodog** transformed back into Robodog. The fins and propeller disappeared inside his body, the wings popped out and the booster rocket fired.

BOOM!

Just as the dogs reached the middle of the lake, the car rose out of the water with Robodog beneath.

WHOOSH!

The dogs looked up as the car flew above them. Robodog delivered it safely at the chief's feet, with a very wet and very relieved officer inside.

CLONK!

"Mission well and truly accomplished!" he chirped.

The chief was amazed. "He's not just a dog! He's a superdog!" She turned to her wife. "Professor! You are a genius! Could you make a hundred of these? A thousand? No, ten thousand!"

"Maybe," she replied. "But this one is super special."

"I thought I was the only one," chirped Robodog.

"You are."

"For now," added the chief.

All the time, perched on top of a roof with a pair of binoculars, was Velma. The cat had been observing Robodog's every move.

"This thing must be destroyed!" she hissed to herself.

"Well done today, Robodog!" said the chief. "You have passed the tests with flying colours!" She reached out a hand to pat his metal head before thinking better of it.

"All in a day's work for Robodog!" said the robot dog. "Welcome to the future of crime fighting!"

"Oh no!" gasped Gristle. "He's even got a catchphrase!"

"Dogs," said the chief, "you have all witnessed something extraordinary today. This brand-new police dog, Robodog, has set the gold standard for you all to follow."

"Which one is Robodog again?" asked Plank.

"And, as such, I have decided that Robodog will be kennelled with the dogs who can learn most from his shining example... THE LOST PATROL!"

"WHAT?!" exclaimed the three.

"It will be your most challenging challenge yet! To turn these three reprobates, the nervy Scarper, the idle Gristle and the silly Plank into model police dogs just like you!"

"Whoever they are," muttered Plank, "I feel sorry for them!"

Scarper and Gristle shook their heads in despair. Plank really was the silliest dog in the world.

ZAP!

From the moment Robodog trundled into the Lost Patrol's shed, fur flew.

It was the messiest place in the whole of the **POLICE DOG SCHOOL**. Despite the chief's strict rules for the dogs to keep the school tidy, the floor was thick with a carpet of:

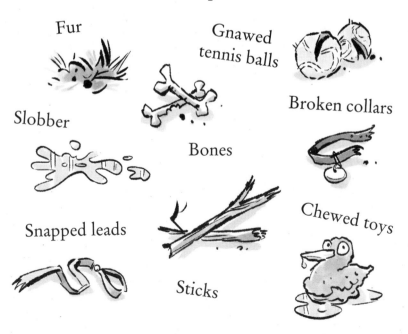

Fur

Gnawed tennis balls

Broken collars

Slobber

Bones

Snapped leads

Chewed toys

Sticks

Torn pages from an
old newspaper

A stolen slipper
(owner unknown)

Robodog trundled into the shed and announced, "This shed is a health hazard! It must be deep-cleaned immediately."

The Lost Patrol protested.

"That slipper won't chew itself!" exclaimed Plank.

"If you don't do any dusting, after the first couple of years, the dust doesn't get any worse!" reasoned Gristle.

"I would love to help, but I am afraid of dirt," added Scarper.

Robodog was having none of it. His laser eye glowed **red,** and beams of light shot out.

ZAP! ZAP! ZAP!

In moments, the offending items were burned to a crisp. All that remained dotted across the floor were little piles of ash.

"NOOO!" cried the three.

"Now, Lost Patrol, I must turn my attention to you!" said Robodog.

The three dogs backed into a corner with

their paws up. They were trying their best to hide behind each other. Were they about to suffer the same fate as their rubbish?

"DON'T BLAST ME! BLAST HIM!" yelled Scarper, pointing to Gristle. "HE'S MUCH MORE BLASTABLE!"

Robodog shook his head. "No. I am not going to blast any of you. I am going to teach all three of you to become the best police dogs you can be!"

"Oh! So that's what we're at school for!" exclaimed Plank. "To become police dogs? No one told me!"

The other two shook their heads. If there were medals for silly dogs, Plank would win gold.

"My name is Robodog. Fellow dogs, please introduce yourselves."

"Well, I am Scarper," began Scarper, "but we are not your fellow dogs."

The other two members of the Lost Patrol stared at him. Where was all this going?

"And why is that?" demanded Robodog.

"You are not a **real** dog!" said Scarper.

The robot dog fell silent. Even his constant *whirrs* and clicks stopped.

"Not a real dog? Does not compute," he said.

"We are **real** dogs. We chase balls, we chew sticks, we dig for bones, we make a mess, we blow off," explained Scarper.

"HA! HA!" laughed Plank and Gristle.

"What is that sound you are making?" asked Robodog.

"Laughter!" exclaimed Gristle. "It is a sound you make at something funny."

"What was funny?" asked Robodog.

"When Scarper said 'blow off'," said Plank. "Blow-offs are always funny!"

"Are they? Why?"

"If you don't know what's funny about blowing off, then you will never, ever, ever be a real dog!" said Scarper.

"Of course I am a dog!" protested Robodog.

"I am Robodog!"

"You are **not** a dog!" said Scarper. "And you never, ever will be!"

Then the strangest thing happened. A drop of oil welled in Robodog's eye.

"What is that?" asked Plank.

"It looks like a tear," replied a surprised Scarper. "But it can't be. Robodog's not even a **real dog!** He can't be sad! It's **impossible!**"

Robodog was feeling something for the first time in his short life. Up to this point, he had only had thoughts. But now something was burning deep inside him. Sadness. It was overwhelming and confusing all at once. Feelings began piling up on top of each other. Suddenly, he felt... ashamed, as if he needed to hide that he was feeling sad. So Robodog did another thing he'd never done before.

He lied.

"MALFUNCTION! MALFUNCTION! MALFUNCTION!" he repeated over and over in his robotic voice.

To add to the performance, he began circling backwards as if he were chasing his own tail.

"MALFUNCTION! MALFUNCTION! MALFUNCTION!"

Robodog bashed into a bowl…

KLANK!

…walloped into a wall…

KLUNK!

…and banged into Plank, who was laid out on the floor in a pool of her slobber.

WHOOMP!

"OOF!"

After creating as much mess as there was before, Robodog trundled out of the shed.

Now there were cats, cats and **more** cats gathered in the city's spooky park at midnight.

Velma had climbed a statue. Perched on its stone head and lit by the silvery moon, she addressed the others. Just as in her household, Velma assumed she was top dog, or at least

top cat.

"Now listen up, cats of **BEDLAM**. As your unelected leader—"

The street cats were furious.

"Why have you called us all here?"

"I could be out chasing rats!"

"Look at her soft fur! What does she know? She's one of them right stuck-up cats that never leave the house."

"**RIIIIAAAAOOOW!**" snarled Velma.

She bared her fangs and her sharp claws pinged out. Now she had their attention.

"Thank you!" she began. "There is a new menace in **BEDLAM!** A menace far worse than any of the master criminals that roam our streets! A menace that will destroy not only our lives, but the lives of **all** cats around the world! If we do nothing, we cats are doomed forever!"

The cats looked around at each other in a state of shock. Except one.

An alley cat with a huge scar across his face stepped out of the shadows.

"What rot!" he snarled.

"Who on earth are you?" demanded Velma.

"You don't know me?"

Velma shook her head.

"I run this city. They call me 'Slash'. You see this scar? I got that from a fight with a pack of wolves."

"What happened?"

"They died. So, darling, nothing and nobody and no one can destroy me. Not even the biggest, baddest dog in the world!"

Velma shook her head again. "Well, I am sorry to be the one to burst your balloon, Slash, but you haven't met Robodog!"

A stunned silence descended on the cats.

"A robot dog?" spluttered Slash.

Velma nodded her head. "The fastest, strongest, smartest dog who ever lived."

"Then that dog must be destroyed!"

"If only it were that simple, Slash," replied Velma. "The problem is: Robodog is indestructible."

The cats fell silent for a moment before a booming voice was heard from the back.

"I will sit on him!"

All turned to look at a mountain of a cat who was lolling in a wheelbarrow, his preferred mode of transport. "I am Pavarotti, and I promise you I can squash him as flat as a pancake. Look, here's one I made earlier!"

With that, he yanked a flattened dog out from under him.

"That won't work in this case, Pavarotti," replied Velma. "The professor who built him has made him bombproof!"

"But is he bumproof?" boomed Pavarotti, much to the amusement of the others.

"TEE! HEE! HEE!"

"I hate to state the obvious," piped up a scraggly old cat, leaning against a tree. "Name's Codger, by the way. But does this robot dog have an **off** button?"

There were murmurs of approval. It did seem like the simplest idea.

"Just switch the blasted thing **off!**"

"Off! Off! Off!"

"Forever!"

"NO! NO! NO!" shouted Velma over the ever-growing chorus of cats. "You turn Robodog off and then someone can just turn him straight back on again. Then we are back to square one. No! Robodog must be destroyed. Forever."

"YES!" cried the cats.

"LET'S ROCK AND ROLL!" shouted Slash.

"WAIT!" shouted Velma from the top of the statue. "We need a plan because we won't be able to get anywhere near the blasted thing."

"Why?" demanded Codger.

"Because right now Robodog is at the **POLICE DOG SCHOOL**."

There were shouts from the cats.

"The **POLICE DOG SCHOOL!**"

"You have to be joking!"

"That's home to a hundred dogs!"

"I am not going anywhere near that place!"

"We'll never get out of there alive!"

Immediately, the cats began slinking off into the night.

"WAIT!" shouted Velma again.

"COME BACK!"

But they just kept on slinking. Soon there were only three remaining: Slash, Pavarotti and Codger.

"DARN!" screamed Velma.

"Don't upset yourself, love. We three are all you need," said Slash.

"All we have to do is get the other dogs out of the school," said Codger.

"But how?" demanded Slash.

"We're cats. We're smart. We must be able to think of something!"

"Especially me," agreed Velma.

There was silence for a moment.

"Food!" piped up Pavarotti.

"Don't say you're hungry again?" asked Slash.

"The great Pavarotti is always hungry. But I know creatures that are even greedier than the greediest cat in the world..."

"DOGS!" cried all four cats in unison.

In moments, a DASTARDLY MASTERPLAN TO DESTROY ROBODOG was hatched.

RATTY THE MOUSE

Alone in the **parade** ground, Robodog came to a stop.

"I must be a real dog!" he said defiantly. "I can bark and chase and roll over…"

"Who are you talking to?" came a voice.

"WHO GOES THERE?" demanded Robodog.

There followed the sound of a whistle.

"WOO-HOO! Down here!" said the voice.

The robot looked down to see a rat climbing out of a storm drain.

"A rat! I must blast it!" said Robodog, his laser-blaster eye protruding, ready to fire.

"I'm not a rat!" lied the rat, raising his paws

in panic. "I am just an unusually large and rather ugly mouse."

"Does not compute!" said Robodog.

"What are you on about now?"

Robodog used his X-ray eye to scan the creature. His verdict was firm but fair. "You do not look, sound or smell anything like a mouse."

"Well, us mouses, I mean mice, come in all **shapes** and sizes, just like you dogs."

This stopped Robodog in his tracks. "You just said I am a dog?"

"Well, what else are you?" spluttered the rat.

"I don't know. The other dogs said I wasn't a real dog... It made me feel sad. A tear welled in my eye."

The rat was, for once, lost for words. He climbed out of the drain and looked the mechanical creature up and down. "Why would anyone say such a thing? Course you are a dog! Just like I am a mouse, right? No blasting needed."

Robodog nodded his head.

"I am Robodog."

"Imaginative name for a robot dog! My name's **Ratty**."

"Strange name for a mouse."

"Oh! That's what I told me mum and dad, but would they listen?"

"I don't know. Would they?"

"Never mind! Look, one thing to remember,

Robodog, is that in this life you can be whatever you want to be."

"What do you mean, **Ratty**?"

"If you wish with all your **heart** to be a dog, then who says you can't be?"

"I don't have a **heart** to wish from," said Robodog sorrowfully. "Maybe that's why the other dogs think I am not real."

"Of course you have a **heart**," replied **Ratty**.

"Do I? I have rockets, and a laser, but I don't know if I have a **heart**."

"If you can feel something, if you can cry like the rest of us, then in there somewhere must be your **heart!**"

With that, he put his grubby little paw on the robot's chest.

"I can feel something else now," said Robodog.

"I can feel something warm and fuzzy."

"That's happiness, I bet. Now you are feeling it, I am feeling it too!"

Robodog thought for a moment. "Maybe I can feel something, but I am still nothing like the other dogs."

"Who wants to be like everyone else? Just like I am not your average mouse, you are not your average dog! That is what makes us both special. Now come on, get back in that shed with your head held high, and get some rest."

"Thank you, **Ratty**!"

"And thank you, Robodog, for not blasting me!"

"Of course!"

"This could be the start of a beautiful friendship," said the rat as he disappeared down the drain.

ONE BILLION DOLLARS!

Robodog had performed so spectacularly in the challenges that the chief decided he was ready to be put to the test on the dark and dangerous streets of **BEDLAM**. So she and the professor took Robodog out of school for the day. This was much to the delight of all the other dogs, who roared their approval, none louder than the Lost Patrol who had been forced to share their shed with him.

"HOORAY!" they cheered as Robodog was whisked away in the back of the Chief of Police's car.

"Good riddance!" said Scarper.

"I hope he never comes back!" added Gristle.

"Who's gone?" asked Plank.

From the back of the car, Robodog saw the city of **BEDLAM** for the first time. It was a gloomy and foreboding place, a city crumbling to the ground – a city that was about to be the scene of the greatest crime ever committed!

One billion dollars was being driven through **BEDLAM**. It was being transferred from the government's printing press, where the money was made, to the city's main bank.

BEDLAM'S villains knew all about it. Villains make it their business to know all about such things – that is why they are the villains.

It was such a colossal amount of money that the president had deemed it too much for the police to guard. So, in his wisdom, he had given the task to the army. It was humiliating for the Chief of Police, but she was also worried that something might go wrong. Someone was sure to try to steal those **one billion dollars.** No one knew these dark and dangerous streets better than the chief, so she wanted to be there in the thick of it with her brand-new secret weapon... ROBODOG!

Along the route where the armoured convoy was travelling, people had lined the streets to catch a glimpse of what was happening. The chief, the professor and Robodog installed themselves on a street corner. A tall general with a chestful of medals spotted the chief and marched right up to her.

"Shame the **BEDLAM** Police Force couldn't be trusted with this, eh, Chief!" he barked. "Thank goodness for the army!"

"Nice to see you too, General," replied the chief.

"I have personally planned this manoeuvre!" he boasted. "The **one billion dollars** has been placed in a tank."

"A tank!"

"You can't take any chances in this city, Chief! And the tank is being escorted by not one, not two, not three..."

"Just tell us how many!" sighed the professor.

"Four armoured vehicles! They are left, right, ahead and behind the tank to create a wall of steel."

"What about an attack from above? Some of **BEDLAM'S** supervillains have been known to take to the air."

"Already thought of that, Chief. Look up there!" The General pointed to the sky where a military helicopter was hovering.

"Mr General, sir!" chirped Robodog.

"Who said that?"

"Down here, Mr General, sir!"

The General looked down. "I thought you were a novelty trash can."

"The cheek!" said the professor.

" General, what about an attack from below?"

The General snorted and shook his head. "Who or what are you?"

"I am Robodog, the future of policing!"

The General burst out laughing. "HA! HA! HA! As if this metal box can take on the baddies

of **BEDLAM!** Have you gone bananas, Chief?"

The lady was too dignified to reply.

"An attack from below! What claptrap!"

"With my supersensory hearing," said Robodog, "I have heard tapping under the ground."

"This thing is hilarious!" snorted The General.

"I can still hear it," said Robodog.

"Robodog might be on to something, General!" said the professor.

"And pigs might fly! Oh! Here comes the convoy now. Right on time," he said, checking his watch. "To the second!"

The armoured vehicles and the tank turned on to the street where the group was waiting.

"Nothing and nobody can stop this convoy!" said The General.

But he was wrong. Wronger than wrong. Wrongwongywoowah!*

Now, let's travel below ground!

The baddies were, as always, one step ahead of the goodies. A giant *leap* ahead was the master criminal known as **MIGHTY MIND**. He was so called because he was the cleverest criminal who'd ever lived. **MIGHTY MIND'S** body had died decades before, but he'd preserved his own mega-brain. That giant brain lived in a glass bowl on wheels.

---

* *This word is even too silly to be in* The Walliamsictionary.

As always, **MIGHTY MIND** was accompanied by his henchperson, **Hammerhands. Hammerhands** was a short, round, unsmiling lady who had lost both her hands in an explosion when she'd used too much dynamite to blow up a safe.

KABOOM!

Now, instead of hands, the lady had giant hammers that could do a lot of DAMAGE.

CLONK!

Despite their peculiar names, **MIGHTY MIND** and **Hammerhands** were the most feared criminal duo in the entire world.

Today the evil pair had their sights set on that one billion dollars. They were going to do anything, however bad, to get their hands (well, hammers) on it.

THE PLAN

MIGHTY MIND'S plan was simple but brilliant. From below ground, **Hammerhands** had been put to work using her hammers. Only allowed the briefest of breaks to have a slurp of tea or use the bathroom, she had bashed the underside of the road until it had CRACKED like an egg. That was what Robodog could hear under the ground with his SUPERSENSORY hearing.

2

The idea was to weaken the road so that when the incredibly heavy tank carrying the **one billion dollars** rode over it, it would collapse.

KERUNCH!

3

The tank would plummet into the sewer.

Then, using sticks of dynamite, **MIGHTY MIND** and **Hammerhands** would blow a hole in the tank and make off with the one billion dollars!

They even had a mini-submarine to escape through the sewers and out into the sea. It was the perfect plan. Or so the wicked duo thought. But they hadn't bargained on **Robodog**!

Now, let's travel above the ground. The General was still boasting.

"You see, Robodog, those **one billion dollars** are completely—"

But before he could say "safe" the tank containing the money completely disappeared.

KERUMBLE!

It had fallen through a giant hole in the road.

THOMP!

The armoured vehicles screeched to a stop.

SCREECH!

The chief gave a knowing look to The General.

"WHAT THE—" he thundered as he ran over to the hole through which his tank had plunged.

"Robbery in progress!" said Robodog, zooming towards the scene of the crime.

"Be careful, my baby!" called the professor.

The chief was flabbergasted. "Did you just call him your 'baby'?"

"It just slipped out!"

Robodog peered down into the deep hole in the road. In the darkness, he could see sparks of light and could hear the sound of something fizzling.

The General had now caught up with Robodog. He was standing right behind him.

"OUT OF MY WAY!" he thundered.

"GET BACK, GENERAL!" shouted Robodog. "THAT'S DYNAMITE!"

But it was too late.

There was a huge explosion underground.

KABOOM!

And a fireball burst through the hole.

WHOOMPH!

A RIVER OF GUNGE

*I*n half a second, Robodog shot out his wings while tipping himself upright.

TWING!

Bravely, he shielded The General as best he could from the explosion.

WHOOMPH!

But they were both blasted backwards.

"ARGH!"

The General hit the road with a BUMP! Robodog landed on top of him.

THUD!

"Get this stupid lump off me!" yelled The General.

The explosion rocked **BEDLAM** like an earthquake. The chief and the professor stumbled towards the pair.

"ROBODOG!" shouted the chief.

"NOOOO!" cried the professor.

"DON'T WORRY ABOUT THIS WALKING TRASH CAN!" boomed The General. "YOU SHOULD BE WORRIED ABOUT ME!"

The ladies went to work, rolling Robodog off the irritating man.

"THIS THING MUST BE DESTROYED!" shouted The General.

"This thing," began the professor, "just saved your life!"

"And now, with any luck," continued the chief, "it will save your **one billion dollars!** Are you all right, Robodog?"

"Yes, Chief!" he chirped, even though he was covered in soot from the blast.

"Excellent! Now after those baddies and those **one billion dollars!**"

Robodog sped back towards the smouldering hole in the road.

W H I R R !

Without a thought for his own safety, Robodog tumbled into the hole.

SPLURGE!

Robodog popped his head out and spotted the giant hole in the side of the tank.

"The one billion dollars are gone!"

Far off in the distance, he spied a mini-submarine powering through the *GUNGE.*

In an instant, his propeller and fins popped out.

WHIRR!

Then a voice from inside the mini-submarine echoed along the sewer.

"HAMMER IT, Hammerhands!"

Hammerhands appeared out of the hatch, brandishing her enormous weapons. She leaped down into the gunge...

SPLURGE!

...and waded through it towards the robot dog.

"I said 'you are under arrest'!" repeated Robodog.

A wicked grin spread across **Hammerhands's** face.

Then she raised her hammer hands high above her head before bringing them down on to Robodog with a mighty...

The force of the blow was so strong that it sent Robodog speeding back down the sewer.

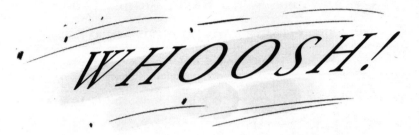

WHOOSH!

For the first time in his life, he felt fear.

"HELP!" he cried as he spun through the gunge.

His voice echoed along the sewers.

"H-E-L-P!"

Of course, no one could hear him so deep underground in the city's sewer system.

Except…

Ratty!

As it was for all the rats of **BEDLAM**, the sewer was his home. When **Ratty** heard Robodog's cry, he was floating in a little cardboard box on top of the gunge, gobbling a piece of cheese. Well, he *hoped* it was cheese.

"H-E-L-P!"

Ratty knew that robotic voice anywhere. It was his new best friend, Robodog! Instantly, he stood up and leaped on to the nearest thing floating on the gunge that would take his weight, and then the next, and then the next: a tin can, a glass bottle, a tennis ball.

"R-O-B-O-D-O-G!" he called out in the darkness.

"R-A-T-T-Y?"

"I AM COMING FOR YOU!"

The sewers were a maze, but **Ratty** knew them like the back of his paw.

After quite a few hops, skips and jumps, **Ratty** found Robodog. The once gleaming robot was now a crumpled mess, bobbing upside down in the gunge.

PLOP!
PLOP!
PLOP!

His metal armour was battered, his propeller was all bent and his fins on one side had snapped off.

"Oh dear," said **Ratty**. "Oh dear! Oh dear!"

"Thank you!" gurgled Robodog, his head below the gunge. He just managed to right himself, so his face was now visible.

"What on earth happened to you?" asked **Ratty**.

"An old lady with hammers for hands sent me flying."

Ratty shrugged. "Not the answer I was expecting, but pray continue…"

"And there was a man barking orders to her from inside their submarine!"

"MIGHTY MIND!" exclaimed **Ratty**.

"You know him?"

"Know him! He is one of the greatest criminal masterminds ever to walk, or rather roll, the streets of this wretched city!"

"Roll?"

"MIGHTY MIND is just a brain."

"Just a brain?"

"Well, a great big brain floating around in a

fish bowl on wheels!"

"This great big brain has just stolen **one billion dollars**! And, right now, he and his henchperson are escaping!"

Ratty thought for a moment. "There is only one way out of this city if you are underground. All the sewerage tunnels lead out into the river. That must be where they are heading. Let's GO!"

With that, **Ratty** leaped on to Robodog's head. But, instead of surging forward, the robot just bobbed about in the gunge. The propeller made a sad gurgling sound. Being bent, the propeller was unable to do any propelling.

SWURGLE!

"MALFUNCTION! MALFUNCTION!"

cried Robodog in exasperation before he gave up. The propeller gurgled to a stop.

"Let me help!" said **Ratty**. "Rats, I mean mice, are stronger than they look!"

The creature jumped off his friend's head and landed in the gunge.

PLOP!

Ratty kicked his little legs as hard as he could, trying to push his metal friend forward, but it was impossible.

"I can't do it!"

"It's not your fault, **Ratty**. It's me! I am useless!" said Robodog.

"Don't be daft!"

"I am not being daft! Real dogs have legs so they can swim. Not a bent propeller and some snapped-off fins!"

"You're special, remember?"

"I don't feel it!"

"Well, you are, and when you are special you

just need to come up with an idea that's special too."

Ratty clambered up on to Robodog's head, placed a couple of his toes in his mouth and let out the loudest whistle.

" **W E E E !** "

The sound echoed along the sewers. Then there was silence for a moment.

"What are we waiting for?" asked Robodog.

"Shush!" shushed **Ratty**.

At first there was a low rumble, then it grew louder and louder and louder until the rumble was deafening. Floating along the gunge came a huddle of rats in an ice-cream container. They were powering themselves along with an electric whisk.

W H I R R !

It was like an outboard motor on a boat.

"Who are they?" asked Robodog.

"Fellow rats, I mean mice."

"You wot?" said a particularly big one.

"Just go with it," hissed **Ratty**. "I will explain later. Friends! This dog here needs a tow!"

"That ain't a dog!" boomed a little one with a deep voice.

"There's no time for all that!" shushed **Ratty**. **"One billion dollars** has gone missing!"

"That's a lot of cheese!" remarked the little one.

"MIGHTY MIND and **Hammerhands** are making off with it now!" added Robodog.

"Throw me your line!" ordered **Ratty**. "We need a tow! To get after them!"

Some rope was thrown from the ship and **Ratty** secured it round Robodog's head.

"Done!"

"Which way now?" asked the big one.

"This way!" exclaimed **Ratty**, pointing down a little side tunnel. "If we go fast enough, we could head the baddies off where the sewer meets the river!" he added.

"Whisk to **super-speed!**" ordered the little one. *WHIRR!*

CATROBATICS

Meanwhile, above ground, a crime spree was occurring.

A cat-crime spree!

Welcome to…

PART ONE OF THE CATS' MASTERPLAN TO DESTROY ROBODOG:

STEAL ALL THE DOG TREATS IN BEDLAM.

On Velma's command, her gang of cats had disguised themselves as a person. They were standing on each other's shoulders like an acrobatics act.

Or catrobatics* act.

---

*See your **Walliamsictionary**. *Available only in bargain bins.*

Pavarotti was on the bottom, then Codger, then Slash, with Velma at the top.

Once on each other's shoulders, the tower of cats dressed in a long coat, a hat and sunglasses.

Velma had cat-burgled the lot from her mistresses' wardrobes.

Now fully in disguise, the tower of cats wobbled into the biggest pet shop in **BEDLAM**. Slash stuffed his paw into a coat pocket, so it looked as if he were holding a gun.

Then Velma, at the top in her hat and dark glasses, gestured for all the dog treats to be handed over.

Clutching the haul in four sets of paws, the tower of cats wobbled out of the shop.

Then they did the same at the next pet shop. And the next. And the next.

Soon Velma and her gang had robbed every single pet shop in the city of dog treats.

All they needed now was a truck. So, when they spotted one idling outside a pet shop making a delivery, the engine still running, the cats leaped in and drove off. Velma was at the steering wheel, Slash was on the accelerator pedal, Pavarotti was on the clutch and brake pedals, and Codger was on the gear stick.

"COME BACK HERE!" shouted the driver.

But the cats were too quick for him. They sped off down the road, crashing into everything in sight:

Being a cat, Velma had never taken her driving test. Come to think of it, she had never had a lesson! Not one!

Now, let's dive down back under the ground, into the depths of **BEDLAM**. Robodog was being towed by rats through a maze of the smaller sewerage tunnels…

"Left! Right! Right again! Watch out for the bend!" called **Ratty**.

Soon they found themselves in the SUPER-SEWER, the widest of all **BEDLAM'S** sewerage tunnels. This one led directly out into the River Ooze, and from there it was a short distance to the ocean. The only chance our **heroes** had of stopping **MIGHTY MIND** and **Hammerhands** making off with those **one billion dollars** was to intercept them before they made it to the river. Once that mini-submarine was in open water, escape was inevitable. The river flowed into the ocean, and from the ocean the criminals could reach anywhere in the world.

After our **heroes** had travelled through miles of dark tunnels, a tiny dot appeared in the distance. The dot became bigger and bigger until it was a bright circle of light.

"We've nearly made it!" exclaimed **Ratty**.

"How do you know we are not too late?" asked Robodog.

"Listen!" said the big one.

The whisk motor engine was switched off and they drifted silently in their ice-cream tub along the river of gunge.

From behind them in the super-sewer came the hum of the mini-submarine.

WHIRR!

"Our shortcut worked! They are moments away," said **Ratty**. "Now we just need to work out how to stop them!"

"WE WILL BOARD THEIR VESSEL AND NIBBLE THEM BOTH TO DEATH!"

proclaimed the little one, much to the delight of the others.

"YES!"

"I know a way!" chirped Robodog. "A way I can bring them in alive!"

"BORING!" cried the rats.

"Spin me round!"

The rats did as they were told, so now Robodog's bottom was facing the circle of light.

"Get back!" he warned.

Then...

THWUCK!

Robodog fired a rope net from his bottom.

It clung to the end of the super-sewer like a spider's web.

TWANG!

"You're a genius!" exclaimed **Ratty**.

"Well, I am not thick!" agreed Robodog.

All this time, **MIGHTY MIND'S** mini-submarine had been surging straight towards them through the gunge.

SPLURGE!

"We need to get out of their way!" cried **Ratty**.

"There isn't time!" shouted the big ugly one.

"Prepare for impact!" called Robodog. "In three, two…"

But before he could say "one", the mini-submarine crashed into them.

THWACK!

Everyone spun towards the net…

TWANG!

…before rebounding at terrific speed, shooting them all back up the super-sewer!

WHOOMPH!

PARACHUTE!

Now the **heroes** and the villains were all flying through the super-sewer, skimming the top of the gunge.

Robodog could see through the porthole of the mini-submarine. There was an expression of panic painted on **Hammerhands's** face. Even **MIGHTY MIND'S** brain was swimming in circles round its bowl. Well, that was hardly surprising, given the circumstances: they were flying backwards through a sewer at one hundred miles an hour!

What the evil duo couldn't see, but our **heroes** could, was that at any moment now they were going to crash into the army tank that had been carrying the **one billion dollars.**

KERBANG!

The stern of the mini-submarine struck the tank's gun.

CRUNCH!

Instantly, the mini-submarine was half the length it had been.

"We're going to hit them!" shouted **Ratty**.

But Robodog was one step ahead.

"Parachute! FIRE!" he chirped.

The parachute shot out of his back.

WHOOMPH!

Robodog, **Ratty** and all the other rats slowed to a gentle stop.

"Thanks, Robodog!" cried the rats.

"And thank *you*, mice!" he replied. "And well done!"

"HELP! WE'RE TRAPPED!" shouted **MIGHTY MIND** from inside the mini-submarine.

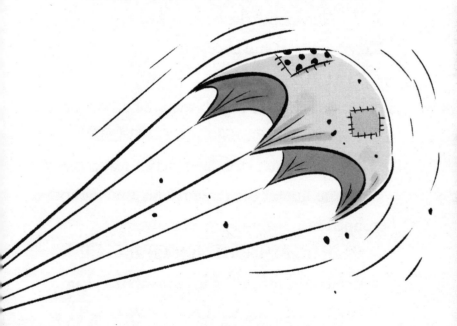

Using his power-drill nose, Robodog cut through the hull.

WHIRR!

Then he plucked the evil duo out with his grabbers. With **Ratty** still perched on his head, he engaged his booster rocket.

BLAST!

They flew out through the tank-sized hole in the road, and above the city of **BEDLAM**.

The huge crowd of citizens who had all been peering down into the hole looked up at the sky. They whooped and cheered.

"HOORAY!"

No one cheered louder than the professor.

"GO, ROBODOG! GO! GO! GO!"

The genius inventor did her cheerleader dance along the line of the crowd. This time nobody stopped her.

"GO, ROBODOG! GO! GO! GO!"

In fact, the crowd joined in with the chant!

"GO, ROBODOG! GO! GO! GO!"

The General looked up at Robodog zooming through the sky, his mouth slack and wide with AMAZEMENT. The chief sidled up to him.

"That one robot dog has done more than your entire army!" teased the chief.

"I'm Robodog. Welcome to the future of crime fighting," said Robodog, much to everyone's delight.

"HOORAY!"

Cameras caught the magic moment.

CLICK!

A legend was born!

Like a true **superhero**, Robodog planted the criminals safely down on the ground.

PLONK!

Instantly, the Chief of Police arrested the pair, though it was unclear how to put handcuffs on a brain floating around in a bowl.

"Excellent work, Robodog," exclaimed the chief.

"Are you hurt?" asked the professor.

"No. No," replied the robot, lying.

Then The General marched up to the group.

"DOGROBOT!" he thundered.

"Not my actual name, but close enough," replied Robodog.

"Where *is* the **one billion dollars?**"

Robodog's head swivelled round like an owl's.

The bag of cash was nowhere to be seen.

"Rats!" exclaimed **Ratty**.

"I will just be one moment, General!" said Robodog, and he flew back down into the sewer with **Ratty** still on his head.

As it happened, the rats hadn't got far. Not least because they were tugging the heaviest sack of money in the world.

"STOP IN THE NAME OF THE LAW!" said the robot dog.

"Oh! Hello, Robodog!" replied the little one. "We were just returning the **one billion dollars** to you, weren't we?"

There was a half-hearted hurrah from the other rats.

"HURRAH!"

"You were going in the wrong direction!" said **Ratty**.

"Were we? Oh! Silly us! Please don't blast us, Robodog! And do make sure this tonne of money is placed safely in the bank and is definitely not all spent on cheese."

In moments, the sack of cash was laid at The General's feet.

"**One billion dollars,** General," chirped Robodog.

"Finally!" exclaimed the man.

He went to pick up the bag.

"Forgive me, General," butted in the chief, "but I have to say the army were just not up to the job!"

"HOW DARE YOU!" he thundered.

"I do dare! I do! This is now a task for the police. Or, rather, one very special police dog! Robodog, ensure the **one billion dollars** is delivered safely to the city bank!"

"Yes, Chief!" chirped Robodog, holding on tightly to the sack with his grabbers.

"Right away, Chief!" added **Ratty**, giving a little salute.

BLAST!

Before The General could protest, the pair were soaring over **BEDLAM**, the sack of money bouncing off the top of the skyscrapers.

BOING! BOING! BOING!

MIDNIGHT FEAST

Above ground, the cats and their stolen truck were speeding towards the **POLICE DOG SCHOOL**.

VROOM!

This was **PART TWO** OF THE CATS' MASTERPLAN TO DESTROY ROBODOG:

> TEMPT ALL THE DOGS OUT OF THE POLICE DOG SCHOOL WITH THE STOLEN TREATS SO ROBODOG WILL BE DEFENCELESS.

Velma was still at the steering wheel, shouting down instructions to her three cat accomplices operating the gear stick and the pedals.

"Clutch! Up to fourth gear! Red light! Accelerate!"

Needless to say, there were countless collisions on the journey.

CRASH! BUMP!
SHUNT!

Before long, it was dark, and the school was in sight. Velma turned off the engine and allowed the truck to roll in silence for the final part of its journey. She didn't want to wake up all the dogs.

So, as quietly as they could, the cats jumped down from the cabin, and tiptoed up to a tree that hung over into the **parade** ground.

With ease, they scaled the tree and leaped down into the school. From the inside, they opened the tall metal gates as quietly as they could. Next, they rolled the truck into place, its back nestling between the gates.

Then, they pulled down the ramp and offloaded all the bags and bags of dog treats.

With their sharp claws, they ripped open the bags.

SCRATCH!

Then they scattered the treats all the way from inside the truck to the end of the **parade** ground.

As she held one of the little brown balls in her paw, Velma sniffed it.

"Disgusting!" she hissed.

Pavarotti popped one in his mouth.

"After the first hundred," he mumbled, chewing, "you do get used to the revolting taste."

Once they had created the world's longest trails of treats, the cats set about silently opening all the doors to the kennels. Inside, the dogs were snoring after a hard day's training.

"ZZZZ!"

The only kennel they missed was the little beaten-up old shed beyond the **parade** ground. That was, of course, home to the Lost Patrol.

Once all the doors were open, the cats raced back to the truck. Pavarotti had the biggest, **boomiest** voice, so he was given the task of calling out…

"TREATS!"

Well, if there is one thing guaranteed to wake up any dog, it's shouting the word "TREATS".

Instantly, all one hundred dogs were wide awake and racing across the **parade** ground, gobbling up as many dog treats as they could.

CHOMP! CHOMP! CHOMP!

This was a midnight feast of epic proportions!
The dogs had never seen so many treats!

It was as if all their dreams had come true at once!

Little did they know it was about to turn into a *NIGHTMARE!*

The trails of treats led directly to the back of the truck. Without a thought

of anything but their bellies, the dogs ran up the ramp and piled in. Soon they were gobbling down the treats on the floor of the truck.

CHOMP! CHOMP! CHOMP!

Once all the dogs were inside, Slash jumped off the roof of the truck and yanked the shutter down as he fell.

SHUNT!

Now the dogs were **trapped**.

"GO! GO! GO!" ordered Slash, slapping the side of the truck, before he leaped back into the cabin.

Codger thrust the vehicle into gear as Pavarotti pushed the clutch.

CRANK!

Pavarotti thumped down on the accelerator pedal.

DUMPH!

Velma steered, smiling a sinister smile.

In the back of the truck, the dogs howled a terrible howl.

"AROO! AROO! AROO!"

But there was no stopping these dastardly cats.

In moments, the truck had disappeared off into the dark of the night.

VROOM!

DOGNAPPED!

The Lost Patrol had missed the whole drama. The three had been fast asleep in their shed the entire time, far away from the action. It was only when Robodog finally returned after his incredible adventure that they woke up to discover what had happened.

"Where are all the other dogs?" demanded Robodog as he rumbled into the shed. The robot dog looked as good as new after the professor's tender loving care at her **LABORATORY** had knocked him back into shape.

Scarper, Gristle and Plank were not pleased to see him, especially at this late hour. It was now the early hours of the morning.

"Oh! Bog off, you walking dustbin!"

"We are trying to sleep!"

"Somebody switch him off!"

Robodog was undeterred. "I just checked, double-checked and triple-checked all the kennels, and they are empty. Why?"

"I know!" piped up Plank. The others looked at her, surprised.

"Yes?"

"Because there are no dogs inside."

The robot dog's voice became louder. "Yes, I know they are empty of dogs, but why?"

"Maybe they all popped out for a pee?" guessed Scarper. There was no way he was going outside in the dark to investigate.

"At exactly the same time?" asked Robodog.

"It's not even light yet!" complained Gristle, yawning. "I need my beauty sleep!"

"RIGHT, LOST PATROL!" barked Robodog. "EVERYONE UP RIGHT NOW!"

Everyone stayed exactly where they were. To add a little glacé cherry on top of the cake of insult, Gristle lifted his leg and let out a bottom banger. One of those very long, slow ones that sounds like a wasp circling down, down, down to its death.

BUZZZZZZZZZZZZZZZZZZZZZZZZZZZZZZZZZ

"Siren! Engage!" chirped Robodog. Instantly, the blue light on his head flashed, and a siren wailed.

The three dogs hated the sound.

"ARGH!"

"STOP!"

"MY EARS! MY POOR FLUFFY EARS!"

"Siren! Louder!" barked Robodog.

WOO-WOO! WOO-WOO! WOO-WOO!

It was now **deafening.**

"All right! All right!" cried Scarper. "You have our attention, Robodog! What is it you want?"

"Siren! Disengage!"

The siren stopped.

"It appears that all the other police dogs have been dognapped!"

"Dognapped?" spluttered Scarper.

"DOGNAPPED?" exclaimed Gristle.

"DOGNAPPED?" cried Plank. "That's terrible." Then she thought for a moment. "Sorry, what does 'dognapped' mean? Does it mean the dogs are all having a nap?"

"NO!" blasted Robodog. "IT MEANS THE DOGS HAVE BEEN TAKEN AGAINST THEIR WILL!"

Plank shook her head. "Truly terrible," she muttered, before a quizzical look crossed her face. "What does 'against their will' mean?"

"It means they didn't want to go."

"Where?"

"I don't know," replied Robodog. "That's what WE need to find out."

The Lost Patrol stared at him. "WE?" the three asked in unison.

Meanwhile, the cats were racing across **BEDLAM** in their stolen truck towards *Fuzz Manor*.

VROOM!

Watch out! Here's **PART THREE** OF THE CATS' MASTERPLAN TO DESTROY ROBODOG:

IMPRISON THE CHIEF AND THE PROFESSOR!

Velma overtook every vehicle and smashed into any that wouldn't get out of her way.

SHUNT!

Soon the truck was being chased by a dozen police cars.

WOO-WOO! WOO-WOO! WOO-WOO!

Velma spun the steering wheel from left to right, knocking them all off the road.

All the time, the dognapped dogs in the back of the truck were howling…

"AR*OOO!* AR*OOO!*"

…as they were hurled around.

Up ahead, a line of police cars had set up a roadblock.

Velma called down to Pavarotti at the accelerator pedal.

"Give me everything you've got, big cat!"

Pavarotti sat on the pedal, and the truck all but took flight.

ZOOM!

It thundered straight towards the roadblock.

"MORE! MORE!"

Codger leaped on top of Pavarotti and the accelerator pedal hit the floor.

ZOOM!

The police officers all leaped out of the way…

ARGH!

…as the truck burst through the line of police cars…

BOOF!

…sending them flying…

WHIZZ!

…and crashing to the ground like tin cans.

CLATTER! CLOTTER! CLUTTER!

Still the truck powered on. Velma was a speed demon. So much so that instead of coming to a steady stop outside **Fuzz Manor** she smashed the truck straight into it.

CRASH!

The whole front of the beautiful old house fell away, crashing to the ground.

TRUMBLE!

The poor chief and professor were rudely awoken in bed as their bedroom wall collapsed in front of their eyes.

"EARTHQUAKE!" shouted the chief, as this was the only reasonable explanation as to why their house was now only half there.

The professor grabbed her wife in terror. "Or have we been hit by a bomb?" she cried.

A huge cloud of dust and debris engulfed them, and the pair coughed and spluttered.

"HUR! HUR!"

Out of the cloud, a familiar figure appeared.

"VELMA?" they both screamed.

The evil cat was now sitting on top of the lorry's cabin, a wicked grin on her face.

"TEE! HEE! HEE!" she sniggered.

SUPERCATS!

"YES!" exclaimed Robodog, back in the Lost Patrol's shed. "WE! All of us must work together to find the dognapped dogs. And I need to introduce you to a little friend who has been helping me fight the baddies!"

Robodog then called out: "You can come in now."

"Are there any dogs in there?" came a voice from the other side of the door.

"Just three!"

"Are you sure it's safe?"

"Yes. Of course it's safe," replied Robodog, before swivelling his head back to the Lost Patrol. "You wouldn't hurt a mouse, would you?"

"A mouse? No!" said Scarper.

"Cute little things," agreed Gristle.

"Never!" cried Plank.

"Good," said Robodog, his head swivelling back round to the door. "You can come in now, **Ratty**!"

The three dogs looked at each other. Even Plank thought it was a strange name for a mouse.

Shyly, **Ratty** tiptoed into the shed. "Hello! I'm **Ratty**!"

The three dogs shared another look.

"I can see you are all going to get along just fine," said Robodog.

"RAT!" howled Scarper.

The three dogs went BANANAS!

They began yelping and chasing the creature all around their shed.

"STOP!" ordered Robodog.

But they wouldn't. The sight of this creature had hurled them headfirst into a frenzy.

"I am just a big ugly mouse!" cried **Ratty**.

231

This did nothing to stop them. They bashed into the walls in their pursuit.

CRASH!

BANG!

WALLOP!

Soon the entire shed collapsed!

THWUMP!

There was nowhere left for **Ratty** to hide, so he leaped on to Robodog's head.

"ROBODOG! TELL THEM TO STOP!" he pleaded.

"STOP!" ordered Robodog. From his eye, a laser blasted as a warning shot.

ZAP!

The ground smouldered.

FIZZLE!

And there was calm, apart from the sound of the three dogs growling.

"GRRRRRRRR!"

All they wanted in life now was to chase that rat. Nothing else mattered in the world, for all eternity and beyond!

"How could you do that to a poor, defenceless mouse?" asked Robodog.

The Lost Patrol looked at each other in disbelief.

"It's a rat!" exclaimed Scarper. "Dogs catch rats! It's just what we do!"

"It's even called **Ratty**!" agreed Gristle. "**Ratty** the rat!"

"Even I know that **Ratty** is a rat, and I am as silly as a goose!" concluded Plank.

"Don't insult geese!" remarked Scarper.

"It's a mouse!" said Robodog.

"What he said," added **Ratty**.

"Now stop this nonsense, Lost Patrol! We have important work to do," added Robodog. "Finding all our fellow dogs!"

"Maybe that's not such a good idea, after all," murmured **Ratty**, eyeing the Lost Patrol warily.

"Fellow dogs?" mocked Scarper.

"Yes," replied Robodog in a flat monotone.

Scarper rolled his eyes. He and his two furry friends all laughed together.

"HA! HA! HA!"

"YOU'RE NO DOG!" exclaimed Scarper.

Robodog looked down at the ground.

"He's more of a dog than you will ever be!" snapped **Ratty**.

The laughter stopped in a heartbeat. The three's grins turned upside down.

Robodog lifted his metal head. "FOLLOW ME!" He was already trundling off. "Lost Patrol! This is your chance to finally become **heroes!**"

"Do we have to?" asked Scarper.

"YES!"

The villains were way ahead of them. They had moved on to **PART FOUR** OF THE CATS' MASTERPLAN TO DESTROY ROBODOG!

OBTAIN SUPERPOWERS!

The cats forced the professor to create special armoured suits for them, just like Robodog's. If the professor didn't do this, then her beloved wife, the chief, would meet a grisly end. This Velma communicated by holding a pen in her paw, and doing a series of drawings, like this...

These drawings were horrific enough for the
professor to understand perfectly!

"NOOOOO!" she cried.

Fuzz Manor squatted on the edge of a
cliff. The chief had been tied to the driving seat
of the truck, and it had been rolled into place
right on the edge.

All that was needed was a tiny little push. Then she and the dogs would plummet to the rocks below.

I told you it was grisly.

The professor was a world-class boffin, so these armoured super-suits came fast. The cats observed the progress down in the **LABORATORY** of *Fuzz Manor,* their claws out in case the professor tried any funny business.

"Soon I will have **deadly powers!** Powers to destroy ROBODOG!" Velma announced to the other three.

"We will all have superpowers!" exclaimed Slash.

"Four against one!" added Codger.

"Robodog won't stand a chance!" boomed Pavarotti.

Then Velma turned to the professor and bared her fangs. **"HISS!"**

"I am going as fast as I can!" protested the

professor as she attached a booster rocket to a washing machine.

Back at the **POLICE DOG SCHOOL**, Robodog was leading the Lost Patrol across the **parade** ground.

"Treats!" exclaimed Scarper. "I can smell them, but I can't see any."

"Not a one!" complained Gristle.

"Did somebody say 'treats'?" piped up Plank.

Robodog was putting the whole thing together in his metal mind like a master detective.

"So a trail of treats was laid to trick the dogs out of their kennels to be dognapped..." he mused.

"Not fair!" muttered Plank. "I wish I'd been dognapped."

"But where were they taken?" asked Robodog.

From his vantage point high up on the robot dog's head, **Ratty's** eyes searched the ground for clues.

"Tyre tracks!" he exclaimed.

"Good work, **Ratty**," replied Robodog. "*Truck* tyre tracks! All we need to do is follow the tracks and we will find out where the dogs were taken! This way!"

With that, Robodog sped off along the road.

WHIRR!

The three members of the Lost Patrol watched him go.

"Well, it's way past my bedtime," said Gristle. "Let me know how you get on. I'll need a lie-in. So I'll catch up with you around lunch! Late lunch!"

The other two shared a look, and then headbutted his butt.

"No! No! Gristle!" said Scarper. "We're all in this together!"

Back at **Fuzz Manor**, the cats' super-suits were finished.

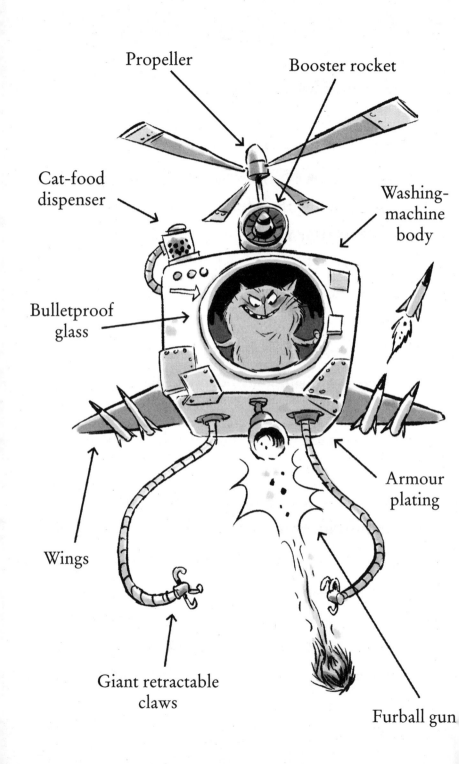

Propeller

Booster rocket

Cat-food dispenser

Washing-machine body

Bulletproof glass

Wings

Armour plating

Giant retractable claws

Furball gun

Sporting wicked grins, the four cats leaped into their suits.

Once inside, they weren't just cats, they were SUPERCATS!

The first thing they did was fly up and out of the **LABORATORY**, carrying the poor professor in their metal claws.

"NOOOO!" she protested, but she was no match for four supercats. They opened the door to the truck and tied her to the passenger seat.

"Not the quiet night in we were hoping for," muttered the chief.

"No!" agreed the professor.

"Now we can destroy Robodog once and for all!" exclaimed Velma. "We will fly to the **POLICE DOG SCHOOL** and blast him to a million metal pieces! FOLLOW ME!"

Velma engaged her booster rocket and zoomed up into the night sky. *BLAST!*

Her three supercats followed her.

BLAST! *BLAST! BLAST!*

Behind them, the police dogs were still stuck in the truck. They howled and howled for someone, anyone, to rescue them. But the only people who could hear were tied to the seats in front.

"AROO! AROO!"

"ROBODOG!" shouted the chief. "We need you! Where are you?"

CREAK!

The truck wobbled over the edge of the cliff. One big gust of wind and they would all be jam, spread over the rocks below.

Meanwhile, Robodog, **Ratty** and the Lost Patrol had reached the edge of the city. The truck's tyre marks ran into the main road that cut right through the centre of **BEDLAM**. The road was a patchwork of tracks, and now it was impossible to work out which way the truck had travelled.

"What now?" asked **Ratty**.

But, before Robodog could answer, four streaks of light lit up the night sky.

"What the…?" said Scarper.

It was only when these streaks grew nearer that Robodog knew what they were.

"CATS!" he exclaimed. "FLYING CATS!"

"NOT JUST FLYING CATS!" shouted Velma from inside her armour-plated flying suit. "SUPERCATS! ROBODOG, WE WERE COMING FOR YOU AT THE **POLICE DOG SCHOOL!** BUT NOW I SEE YOU HAVE SAVED US THE TROUBLE OF GOING ALL THE WAY THERE! PREPARE TO MEET THY DOOM!"

With that, she shot a missile from her super-suit.

ZOOM!

It flew straight at the dogs on the ground!

REVENGE

Robodog had to think fast.

"LEAP ON MY BACK!" he shouted
to the other dogs.

Scarper, Gristle and Plank did as they were
told.

The dogs, plus **Ratty**, shot up into the sky,
just as the rocket exploded.

KABOOM!

"OW!" screamed Gristle.
"My bottom hair just got singed!"

Indeed, it had. It was
smoking. But right now this
was the least of their worries.
Four deadly supercats were
out to destroy them.

More missiles were launched.

WHOOSH!

WHOOSH!

WHOOSH!

"Hold on tight!" ordered Robodog
as he zoomed out of their way.

WHIZZ!

The rockets struck buildings all around them,
exploding in balls of fire.

KABOOM!

KABOOM!

KABOOM!

"WHY?" shouted Robodog. "Why are you doing this? You will destroy the whole of **BEDLAM!**"

"I don't care!" shouted Velma. "Let it burn to the ground! All that matters is that you are destroyed with it, Robodog!"

"But I thought we were friends!"

"FRIENDS?" spat the cat. "*FRIENDS?* Cats loathe dogs with every fibre of their being, and what could be worse than a dog with superpowers!"

"A cat with superpowers?" guessed Scarper, clinging on to Robodog's back for dear life.

"Exactly!" hissed Velma.

"Where are the other dogs?" demanded Robodog.

"About to meet their doom on the edge of a cliff with your precious mummies!"

"NO!" cried Robodog. "Please! I beg you not to hurt them!"

"Why do you care?"

Robodog puzzled over this for a moment. But the answer was obvious. "I love them!"

Velma scoffed. "You are made of metal! You are incapable of love!"

"No, it is **you** who is incapable of love!" shouted **Ratty**.

"Don't worry, little one," purred Velma. "You are about to die too. Now, supercats, on my command, shoot your furballs. FIRE!"

All four fired giant furballs at the dogs.

WHIZZ!

WHIZZ!

WHIZZ!

WHIZZ!

The furballs all expanded on impact, covering every millimetre of the dogs. Thick damp cat hair had enveloped our **heroes** in one giant cocoon. Now it was impossible for Robodog to fly.

"PREPARE FOR CRASH-LANDING!" he exclaimed.

"NOOOOOOOOOOOO!" cried the others, and they found themselves tumbling towards the ground.

"Let's chew our way out!" cried **Ratty**.

"I am not putting a cat's furball in my mouth!" shouted Scarper.

"It's that or die!" replied Robodog.

With his laser, he began cutting a hole in the cocoon.

All the others used their mouths.

"It's disgusting!" moaned Scarper, mouth full of fur.

"Oh, shut up and munch!" shouted Gristle.

"I quite like the taste!" added Plank.

Seconds before they were about to hit the ground, the furball cocoon had been cut into two. It fell away as Robodog swooped up and the gang soared into the sky.

"WE'RE BACK IN THE GAME!" exclaimed Robodog.

"And now it is time for… REVENGE!" added **Ratty**. "One by one, we can take them out."

"For dinner?" asked Plank.

"No. Not for dinner!" snapped Robodog. "We must stop them! I will swoop down low over that one there…" he said, pointing to Pavarotti. Pavarotti had a much bigger super-suit than the other cats. It was made from an industrial-sized washing machine.

"When the moment is right, I will shout JUMP! And, Scarper, you leap off and bring him down!"

"Why me?" he replied, trembling.

"You are the nimblest, and the only one who can make the leap!"

"But—" protested Scarper.

"No buts!"

"But I could die!"

"How much better to die a **hero** than live a coward?" said **Ratty**.

Scarper thought for a moment. "I would be perfectly happy living a coward actually!"

"JUMP!" shouted Robodog.

Scarper shut his eyes tight and leaped off Robodog's back in the direction of Pavarotti.

Without a parachute, he dropped like a stone.

WHOOSH!

He crashed on to Pavarotti's back. There was a mid-air fight, though all that Scarper managed was to shut his eyes and slap.

Fittingly for Pavarotti's namesake (the famous Italian opera singer), the pair spiralled down towards a pizzeria. They crashed through the window.

SMASH!

The cat's super-suit broke into pieces as it skimmed across the restaurant.

CRASH! BANG! WALLOP!

And Pavarotti landed in a huge vat of tomato sauce.

"MAMMA MIA!" cried the cat.
He didn't like being drenched in tomato sauce one bit.

Just as Scarper was about to help himself to a huge slice of pepperoni pizza, he was whisked up into the air by his tail.

"What the…?"

Gristle had grabbed on to him and hoisted his friend on to Robodog's back.

Robodog chirped, "Well done, Scarper. One down! Three to go!"

But if the gang had thought of celebrating, it was far too soon. Slash was determined to beat these dogs at their own game. In his super-suit, he swooped down low over them and landed right on Robodog's back.

CLUNK!

Metal hit metal.

Then the cat stood up on his metal legs and wrestled with the three dogs and one rat.

"He's going to throw us off!" shouted Gristle.

"Prepare to die, doggies!" hissed Slash.

"No dog is dying on my watch," said Robodog.

He swooped towards a bridge that stretched over the river.

"Get down!" he shouted up.

"Like get down and boogie?" asked Plank.

"NO! DUCK!"

"A duck? Where?"

"Get your head down, for goodness' sake!" ordered Robodog.

The dogs did what they were told, and Robodog zoomed just under the arch of the bridge.

WHOOSH!

He narrowly missed hitting the bridge, but Slash's head did not.

CLONK!

Slash was knocked off the back of Robodog and tumbled down into the River Ooze.

SPLASH!

"ARGH!"

he cried as he
hit the filthy
brown water.

Still in his washing-machine super-suit, the flow of the river swept him off towards the ocean.

SWOOSH!

As the dogs watched him disappear downriver, an explosion went off above their heads.

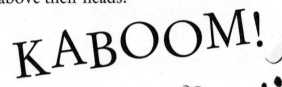

KABOOM!

And another!

KABOOM!

And another!

KABOOM!

Missiles from the other cats must have hit the bridge, as it was now collapsing into the water.

SPLOOSH!

Huge chunks of concrete were spinning through the air.

WHOOSH!

Then one struck Robodog.

THUNK!

It sent him and his friends spiralling down towards the river.

BEDLAM'S BIGGEST BADDIES

Our **heroes** hit the filthy water with a gigantic splash.

SPLOOSH!

"**Submarobodog** mode! Engage!" chirped Robodog.

Immediately, the fins popped out and the propeller whirred.

CLICK! *WHIRR!*

With **Ratty**, Gristle, Scarper and Plank holding on tighter than ever, Robodog powered beneath the surface. All around them huge chunks of the bridge fell...

…sinking to the riverbed.

Robodog sped on until they were well clear of the falling bridge. The robot could stay underwater for hours, but the others would need to take a gulp of air at any second. Above the surface of the river, Robodog could spy one of the supercats hovering overhead. No doubt it was waiting to see if the dogs had drowned or not.

Robodog stopped still under the water so as not to be detected, but the bubbles of air coming from the others were a dead giveaway.

BUBBLE! BUBBLE! BUBBLE!

Spying the bubbles, Codger pressed a button to fire a missile into the water and blast the dogs to oblivion!

BOOM!

Plank couldn't hold her breath any longer. As she scrambled up towards the surface, she pushed away from Robodog's back with her paw – and accidentally struck a button.

CLUNK!

It was the booster-rocket button.

Suddenly, they were all surging up out of the river and straight towards Codger.

The rocket exploded
under them…

KABOOM!

as Robodog's nose
struck Codger.

KERTHUNK!

At once, they were all
soaring into the sky.

WHOOSH!

"STOP!" screamed
Codger.

But Plank's paw was
stuck on the booster-
rocket button. They
couldn't stop. Soon
they'd shot high above
the clouds and were
hurtling into

OUTER SPACE!

"BOOSTER ROCKET DISENGAGE!"

ordered Robodog. But with the button pressed down it couldn't.

I don't know if you have ever been into outer space, but it is ice-cold up there! You definitely need a jumper.

"P-p-please t-t-turn th-that th-thing off-ff-ff!"

spluttered **Ratty**, his teeth chattering.

"Oh, was that me? **Oops!**"

The dog took her paw off the button and immediately Robodog stopped. However, Codger had been pushed so far so fast that he kept on going.

WHIZZ!

The cat was on a **collision course** with the moon!

"I'LL GET YOU!"

he yelled from inside his super-suit as he spun off.

Eventually, he hit the moon with a

CRUNCH!

"OOF!"

His super-suit was crumpled to pieces.

Meanwhile, our **heroes** were falling back to Earth. The intense cold was immediately replaced by the intense heat created when re-entering the Earth's atmosphere.

"OOOOH!" they cried.

Robodog swooped down into a large fountain in **BEDLAM'S** main square.

SIZZLE!

They all dipped their burning bottoms into the cool water.

"AH!" they sighed together.

The relief, however, was short-lived, as a shadow loomed over them.

"VELMA!" cried Robodog.

The evil cat was hovering overhead.

"Before you all meet your end, let me introduce you to some friends of mine I just freed from jail!"

Now, shadowy figures appeared out of the gloom.

It was **MIGHTY MIND** and **Hammerhands!**

"So, we meet again, Robodog!" said the giant brain in the bowl as his henchperson wheeled him closer.

"I don't know what you are going to do," began Plank. "I imagine it is something quite bad, but do you mind holding on a moment? My bottom is still sizzling."

"Hammerhands!" said the brain.

The henchperson knew exactly what to do. **Hammerhands** rubbed her hammer hands together at terrific speed until they glowed red and sparks flew off them.

SPICKLE!

They were now boiling hot, and she placed them on the dog's bottom.

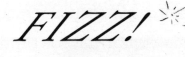

FIZZ!

"OOOWWWEEE!" howled Plank. Her bottom now glowed bright red.

"You've made her look like a baboon!" complained Gristle.

"HUH! HUH! HUH!" snorted the baddies, Velma the loudest.

Although Gristle was the world's idlest dog,

seeing his friend suffering lit a burning energy within him. With all his strength, he made a death-defying leap at **Hammerhands.**

WHOOSH!

"GRRRR!" growled Gristle.

However, mid-flight, Velma shot a furball at him.

BLAST!

The furball cocooned him in an instant. Unable to move a muscle, Gristle fell to the ground with a

THUMP!

"You see!" proclaimed Velma. "I am all-powerful!"

"HELP!" came a muffled voice.

"Who said that?" asked Plank.

"Me – Gristle!" came the voice again. "I am

trapped in this furball cocoon."

"Oh yes. How is it?"

"I'll be honest. Not great!"

"STAND BACK!" boomed Robodog. He shot a laser out of his eye.

The red beam cut through the cocoon, and in moments Gristle was free.

"Thanks!" said the dog.

"You are just a cat in a washing machine!" said **Ratty**, shaking his paw at Velma. "Don't get too big for your boots!"

"Oh! But I have an army. An army of baddies. When I blew a hole in **BEDLAM** City Jail just now, I set *every* dastardly criminal free! Soon I will be able to not just destroy you, Robodog, and all the other dogs on the planet, but I will be able to RULE THE WORLD!"

"Oh no!" said **Ratty**. "These supervillains always go bananas!"

Now, from all around the fountain, more shadowy figures stepped out of the gloom. They were **BEDLAM'S** BIGGEST BADDIES!

As they formed a ring of steel round our **heroes**, Velma purred, "You see, dogs, there is no escape! You are all... *DOOMED!"*

OUTNUMBERED

Our **heroes** were no match for these supervillains. The dogs, the rat and even the robot were all quaking with fear as they were encircled. One of them even accidentally let off a little bottom squeaker…

PFT!

…but it was hardly the time to begin arguing about who had done it.

Dr Stench opened her mouth wide and breathed a green cloud of putrid gas over them.

WHOOSH!

The Ice Queen reached out her icy finger to freeze them forever.

"GET AWAY FROM ME!"

MIGHTY MIND swam around in his bowl like a jellyfish.

"I am just thinking of something particularly evil! Give me a moment!"

The Tickle Monster stretched out his long arms towards them, ready to tickle them to death.

"NOOOO!"

The Masked Honker turned round and shot a fireball at them.

WHOOMPH!

Hammerhands clonked her giant hammer hands together menacingly.

CLONK!

The Chocolatier opened the biggest box of chocolates you had ever seen.

"Help yourself! Just beware the coffee-flavoured ones!"

"No! NO! Not the coffee-flavoured ones!"

THE TWO-HEADED OGRE was too busy arguing with itself.

"I am going to destroy them!"

"No! *I* am!"

"I'll destroy you in a minute!"

Professor Squid lunged towards them waving his arms, ready to fire **black ink** into their eyes.

SQUIRT!

The Politician, who was covered in dust and cobwebs, was waffling on about something or other.

"At the end of the day, when all is said and done, what this once-great city of ours needs is… BLAH! BLAH! BLAH!"

"ZZZZ! ZZZZ! ZZZZ!"

It was all but impossible to stay awake!

Big Bad Bob thumped the ground with his giant fists, causing a mini-earthquake.

RUMBLE!

The **Wicked Headmistress** stepped forward, holding a pile of exercise books.

"I want this homework handed in first thing in the morning, or you will all be held in detention until the end of time!"

"NOOOOOOOOO!"

THE GIANT WORM didn't really do anything, but it didn't have to. It was a giant worm, for goodness' sake!

"We're outnumbered! Our only chance is to outwit them!" said Robodog.

"Well, it's been nice knowing you all, but I have to scarper," whispered Scarper.

"I wish I'd stayed in bed," muttered Gristle.

"What does 'outwit' mean?" asked Plank.

"I know I am the biggest and strongest of us all," began **Ratty**, "but this time I am with Robodog all the way. We have to use our brains!"

"Our what?" said Plank.

Being such a small creature, **Ratty** had always had to use his wits to survive. His brain was spinning with ideas, until he arrived at a particularly brilliant one.

PING!

One he was sure would get the better of these baddies.

"HISS!"

The baddies all took a step closer to our **heroes** and loomed over them, arms outstretched.

Ratty put his paw up. "So sorry. I hate to

be a party pooper, but I have a quick question, Velma!"

"WHAT?" demanded the cat.

"Well, when you said you are going to rule the world, did you mean just you?"

"Well," began Velma, "I will be in charge, obviously, but..."

"But you are just a cat!" said Gristle.

"How dare you!" thundered Velma.

"He does dare! He does!" added Scarper.

"Sorry," interrupted **MIGHTY MIND** from his bowl. "I am so clever, and my brain is so big, that I do speak Cat, Dog and Rat. I must say, the dogs and the rat have a point. I mean, it would be a bit embarrassing if I, the greatest criminal mastermind the world has ever known, was taking orders from a mere moggy!"

There were murmurs of agreement from the other supervillains.

"I don't mind!" said one of the ogre's heads.

"I do!" said the other.

"SILENCE!" ordered Velma. "I freed you all from jail, remember? I deserve to be in charge! I, and I alone, will rule the world forever!"

"Oh! Now it's forever!" said **Ratty**. "Totally and utterly BANANAS!"

"I will translate the cat's speech!" said **MIGHTY MIND**.

As soon as he had, all the baddies burst into life.

"I loved it in jail."

"Three hot meals a day."

"Scrabble night on Thursdays."

"Me and my second head didn't even get a chance to settle in before we were sprung out!"

"And I've been digging a tunnel to escape. Ten years it took me! Now that turns out to have been a complete waste of time!"

Velma was fuming. The round window on her washing machine super-suit steamed up. A little windscreen wiper began shuffling left and right to clear it.

SQUEAK! SQUEAK!

"**HISS!**" she hissed, spraying some spit on to the window.

The little windscreen wipers made their pitiful sound again.

SQUEAK! SQUEAK!

"Just about this whole 'who is going to rule the world' thing," continued **MIGHTY MIND**, "as the baddest baddie of all the baddies, I feel I should do it. All those in favour say 'aye'. AYE! That's settled then!"

The supervillains were in uproar.

"NO!"

"NEVER!"

"NOT YOU EVER!"

"*I* WILL RULE THE WORLD!"

"NO, *ME!*"

"ME!"

"WHAT THIS COUNTRY NEEDS… BLAH! BLAH! BLAH!"

Hammerhands was a woman of few

words, so instead of speaking she banged her boss's glass bowl with her hammer hands.

CRACK!

The bowl shattered and then broke into a billion pieces. The mega-brain slurped out on to the ground.

SPLURGE!

"NOOOOO!" he cried.

Hammerhands ran over to try to scoop **MIGHTY MIND** up, but her hammer hands were no use for that.

The brain disappeared down a drain.

GURGLE!

"HELP!" called out **MIGHTY MIND.** But it was too late. He was being swept away on a river of gunk in the city's sewer.

Hammerhands burst into floods of tears.

"BOO! HOO! HOO!"

She lifted her hands up to her head in anguish and managed to knock herself out.

CLONK!

Hammerhands toppled to the ground with a mighty THUMP!

"So, who is the baddest of all the baddies?" asked Robodog, giving a wink to his fellow dogs. He knew this would wind them up something rotten.

"I AM THE BADDEST!"

"NO! I AM THE BADDEST!"

"I AM THE BADDEST OF THE BAD!"

"I AM THE BADDIE ALL THE OTHER BADDIES, EVEN

THE REALLY BAD ONES, AGREE IS
THE BADDIEST BADDIE THAT EVER
BADDIED!"

Voices were raised. Baddies sized up to baddies.
There was even some pushing and shoving and a
bit of poking.

"There's only one way to settle this!" piped
up Plank. "FIGHT!"

"Genius, Plank!" shouted Robodog.
"FIGHT!"

Immediately, the biggest brawl broke out
between the baddies.

AND FIGHT THEY DID!

Professor Squid's ink was squirted in eyes!

SQUIRT!

"ARGH!"

Great balls of flaming farts were fired from **the Masked Honker's** bottom.

WHOOMPH!

WHOOMPH!

WHOOMPH!

A huge deadly cloud of green gas from **Dr Stench** made all the baddies cough and splutter.

"EURGH!"

The **Wicked Headmistress** began throwing exercise books at everyone's heads.

CLONK! CLONK! CLONK!

"HOMEWORK! HOMEWORK! HOMEWORK!"

The Ice Queen turned *THE GIANT WORM* to ice! It now looked like a giant ice pop!

CRACK!

The Politician was forced to eat one of the Chocolatier's coffee-flavoured chocolates and fell to the ground, frothing at the mouth.

"GURGLE!"

The Tickle Monster tried to tickle **Big Bad Bob** to death.

"HA! HA! HA!"

But all that happened to **Big Bad Bob** was that a little bit of Wee came out.

As for **THE TWO-HEADED OGRE,** it fought itself.

"TAKE THAT!" "NO! TAKE THAT!" KAPOW!

THWACK!

The baddies' brawl was so big that the goodies all took their chance to slink away into the night. Now they had to rescue their fellow dogs!

SPIN CYCLE

Flying over **BEDLAM** on Robodog's back, the gang arrived at **Fuzz Manor** in no time.

"ROBODOG!" exclaimed the chief and the professor at seeing him light up the night sky. They were still tied to the seats of the truck that was swinging up and down on the edge of the cliff like a see-saw.

Robodog hovered level with the truck.

Without thinking, **Ratty** leaped off the robot dog's back and on to the bonnet of the truck.

CLINK!

"I will save you!" he called out heroically, longing for a piece of the action.

Ratty was only light, but he was heavy enough to send the truck plummeting to the rocks below.

"NOOOOOO!" screamed the two ladies.

"*AROOOOOOO!*" howled the dogs.

"SORRY!" screamed **Ratty**.

WHOOSH! went the truck as it fell through the air.

Ratty slipped off the bonnet and screamed as he plummeted too.

"ARGH!"

"HOLD ON TIGHT!" ordered Robodog. "BOOSTER ROCKET: FIRE!"

BLAST!

With the Lost Patrol clinging on, Robodog swooped down at the speed of sound. "ELECTRO-MAGNET: ENGAGE!"

It popped out of his tummy and caught the front of the truck.

CLONK!

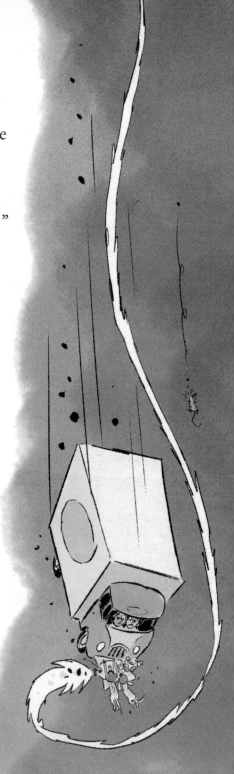

That still left **Ratty** falling to his death.

Gristle opened his mouth and chomped on the rat's tail as he hurtled past...

CHOMP!

...only just saving him from becoming rat juice on the rocks below.

"PHEW!" said **Ratty**. "Thanks! I really wanted to be in a sequel to this story if there is one!"

Then Robodog flew up the side of the cliff and deposited the truck safely in the garden of the country house.

The Lost Patrol leaped off Robodog and set about liberating their fellow dogs from the truck. They howled with delight at being free at last.

"AROO!"

Many charged straight to a tree for a much-needed pee after all that time locked up.

PSSSSSSSS!

With all those dogs sniffing around, **Ratty** thought it best to keep out of sight. So he scaled a birdbath and watched with pride as the happy scene unfolded.

"AH!" he cooed.

After Robodog zapped their ropes with his laser eye...

ZAP! ZAP!

...the chief and the professor leaped out of the truck and embraced Robodog. It didn't matter that he was made of metal – they hugged him as tightly as they could.

"Thank goodness you came back," spluttered the chief.

"You would not believe what happened!" added the professor.

"Oh! I know," said Robodog. "But there is no time to lose. Velma let all of **BEDLAM'S** biggest baddies out of jail!"

"That cat did *what*?!" exclaimed the chief.

Suddenly, all the dogs gathered round to listen.

"So, we need to work together to find them, arrest them and put them back in jail where they belong!" proclaimed Robodog. "At the moment, they're distracted by fighting each other, but that may not last forever."

There were howls of agreement from the dogs.

"AROO!"

"Especially Velma!" piped up **Ratty** from the birdbath. "She needs to be put in jail forever!"

All eyes turned to the rodent. There was a brief moment of calm before all the dogs charged towards him.

"WOOF! WOOF! WOOF!"

They leaped up on their back legs to try to reach him.

"WOOF! WOOF! WOOF!"

"PLEASE! STOP!" shouted Robodog over the din.

Eventually, the dogs fell silent, save for a few whimpers.

"This is my friend **Ratty**. He's a mouse."

"A what?" came a voice from the back.

"You heard me, a mouse. And you are all to leave him be."

"Can't we just play football with him?" came another voice.

"NO! We wouldn't be here now if it wasn't for **Ratty**. He is a **hero!**"

There were murmurs of disappointment from the dogs.

"NOW WHO WANTS TO CATCH SOME BADDIES?" heralded Robodog.

Barks of approval rang out.

"WOOF! woof! WOOF!"

"THEN FOLLOW ME!"

Spurred on by the thrill of adventure, the dogs made it to **BEDLAM** in no time. The fight between the baddies was finally coming to an end. All the villains, bar one, were collapsed on the ground, exhausted. This corner of **BEDLAM** had been destroyed in the epic fight. As it turned out, there was just one baddie still standing. **THE TWO-HEADED OGRE**, of course. It was still punching itself in the faces.

WHACK!　　WHACK!

WHACK!

The ogre wobbled.

There was one more punch.

WHACK!

Before it too fell to the ground.

THUD!

It was easy pickings for the police dogs. In teams of three, they dragged the baddies one by one back to **BEDLAM** City Jail.

"*GRRR!*"

Robodog took great pleasure in being entrusted to heave Velma all the way to the jail! Just as they reached the front door, the professor tried to open the super-suit to take Velma out of it so she would fit through. But as soon as she did the cat's eyes opened wide.

"**HISS!**" she hissed.

"VELMA!" exclaimed the professor.

"I was only pretending to be knocked out!" said the cat. "Now I am going to blast you all to oblivion!"

With that, Velma started aiming her last rocket right at the group.

"What should we do, Professor?" asked Robodog as all the dogs put their paws up in surrender.

"I don't know!" cried the professor. "I mostly design washing machines, not supervillain suits!"

However, the two did look similar.

"That's it!" exclaimed Robodog. "Let's put it

on a spin cycle!"

"YES!" agreed **Ratty**.

He leaped off the robot's back and pressed a button on Velma's super-suit.

Immediately, the cat began to spin inside the suit. Slowly at first, then faster and faster and faster.

WHIZZZZ!

"AAAARRRRGH!" she cried.

But nobody could help her now.
She spun and she spun and she spun.

WHIZZZ!

She spun so fast she took off.

WHOOSH!

She spun up through the air. She
spun above the clouds. She spun
into outer space. She only stopped
spunning – oh, I mean spinning –
when she hit the moon, landing
right on top of Codger.

KLUNK!

Down on
Planet Earth,
the dogs let out
a massive cheer.

"WOOF!"

With all the baddies back in **BEDLAM** City Jail, the chief turned to address the dogs. "Well done, dogs!" she began. "Tonight, each and every one of you has proved that you are a **hero!**"

"**WOOF!**"

"I have decided that first thing tomorrow morning will be your passing-out **parade!**"

The dogs couldn't believe it.

"Tonight, all of you have passed your tests with flying colours, especially the Lost Patrol, who will be awarded special medals for their bravery!"

"**WOOF!**"

"But the biggest thanks has to go to... ROBODOG!"

"**WOOF!**"

agreed all the other dogs.

The chief, the professor and Robodog embraced.

A little drop of oil welled in the robot's eye.

"I am not sad. I don't know why I am crying," he said.

"I do," said the professor, wiping away her own tears. "It's because you are happy."

"Oh no!" said **Ratty**, bursting into tears. "Now you've got me going! BOO! HOO! HOO!"

PASSING-OUT PARADE

The passing-out **parade** went perfectly. All the recruits were officially made police dogs, ready for immediate duty. The professor sat proudly in the front row, surrounded by uniformed police officers all eager to be paired up with these heroic dogs.

The chief was standing on a stage that had little walkways up and down for the dogs. Each dog shook their paw with the chief before making their way back to the group. After the hundred dogs had been welcomed to the police force with rapturous applause, the chief turned her attention to an even more special group.

She beamed as she announced, "Now it is time for me to award the highest honour that can be bestowed on a police dog. These dogs used to be known as the Lost Patrol…"

As she continued her speech, the three dogs looked ill at ease.

"We don't deserve any medals. I'm a coward," said Scarper.

"And I'm lazy," added Gristle.

"And I'm the silly one, aren't I?" asked Plank. "I never can remember."

Ratty leaped off Robodog's back and addressed them one by one: "You are none of those things. Scarper, you showed great bravery out there. You fought Pavarotti, the biggest, baddest cat of them all. Nothing cowardly about that. You, Gristle, there is nothing lazy about making a death-defying leap to defend your friend. And as for you, Plank, you were the one who told the baddies that the only way they could settle their arguments was with a fight. Which meant *we* didn't have to fight them! How smart is that?"

"Well said, **Ratty!**" agreed Robodog. "Enjoy your medals! You have earned them."

Meanwhile, the chief was coming to the end of her speech. "So please join me in welcoming to the stage the no-longer Lost Patrol, but three shining examples of bravery, dedication and intelligence: Scarper, Gristle and Plank!"

The dogs smiled over at Robodog and **Ratty** as gold medals were placed round their necks.

"Now it is time for our newest recruit, and the creation of my brilliant and beautiful wife, the professor, to come to the stage to officially be made a police dog. Please be upstanding for Robodog…"

All those in the **parade** ground took to their feet to give this heroic robot the ovation he deserved.

"Robodog?" called out the chief.

"ROBODOG?"

But the robot was nowhere to be seen.

"**Ratty?**" called out the chief. "Where has he gone?"

But all the rat could do was shrug. "Search me!"

LOVE

The chief and the professor arrived back at their country house that afternoon, utterly downcast. The big moment the chief had planned for her wife's genius creation had been ruined. What's more, they were feeling a deep sense of loss. They had lost a part of the family. So you can imagine their shock when they walked into their living room to see Robodog sitting by the fire!

"ROBODOG!" they exclaimed.

They rushed over and wrapped their arms round him.

"We were so worried about you," said the professor.

"You missed the passing-out **parade!**" added the chief.

"I know," began the robot, "but I have been thinking. And feeling."

"Feeling?" asked the professor.

"Yes. Feeling. And I learned in my short life that feelings go deeper than thoughts. Well, I know this must sound ridiculous..."

"Tell us!" implored the chief.

"...but I don't want to be a police dog any more. I just want to be your dog. Your pet."

"But why," said the chief, "when you could be the greatest police dog in the history of the world?"

"Because I want to feel something that real dogs do."

"What's that?" asked the chief.

"I think I know," said the professor with a smile.

"Well..." said the robot, "this might sound silly, but I suppose... what I want... is love."

"Love?"

"Yes. If I can love and be loved, then I *must*

be a real dog."

The professor looked at the chief, and raised her eyebrows.

"We couldn't love you more, Robodog," said the chief.

"And I love you both."

At last. He was a real dog.

*T*hat night, while Robodog was asleep at the end of his mothers' bed, he was awoken by a tap on the window. It was only when the dog pulled back the curtains that he knew who it was. **Ratty**.

Robodog opened the window.

"What do you want at this hour?" asked the dog. "It's way past midnight!"

"Did it go all right with the two ladies?"

"Yes," said the dog, beaming.

"I told you it would. I covered for you at the **parade** ground good and proper. Didn't give the game away."

"I was sure they would have heard me burrowing under the ground."

"Not a peep!"

"So why are you here?"

Ratty smiled. "Well, I know I'm just a lowly rat, I mean, mouse…"

"You don't need to pretend with me! I knew all along!"

"Rat, then!" said **Ratty**. "My secret's out!" The dog chuckled.

"Shush!" shushed the rat. "You'll wake up the parents!"

"Oh yes!"

"Well, I know I'm just a lowly rat, but I rather liked all that police-dog nonsense."

The dog smiled. "Me too!"

"I thought you'd say that, and I wondered…"

"Yes?" replied the dog eagerly.

"Well, I wondered if you fancied a little midnight police patrol now and again."

"Now?"

"Yes! Now. And again tomorrow night. And the night after that. And the night after that."

"YES!" replied the dog.

"Excellent! The streets of **BEDLAM** need keeping safe!"

"By Robodog, the future of crime fighting!"

"And his trusty sidekick, **Ratty** the rat."

"Hop on!" said the dog.

The rat grinned from dirty ear to dirty ear and leaped on to his best friend's back.

"Let's catch us some baddies!" said **Ratty**.

"I can't think of anything better!" replied Robodog.

He rose off the floor, and then shot out of the window, faster than a speeding bullet.

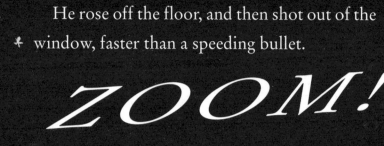

ZOOM!

They blazed across the inky black sky, the crime-riddled city of **BEDLAM** laid out beneath them.

Adventure was calling.

Tonight, and forever.